G000108367

Rib Bone Jack:
Smuggler's Pride

By

John Williamson

Copyright © 2019 John Williamson

All rights reserved

ISBN: 9781705551776

Note to readers

This book is written with an adult audience in mind and does contain some swearing and violence for the purposes of authenticity.

Though set in the Napoleonic war era, it doesn't claim to be in any way historically accurate and is entirely a work of fiction.

Other books in the series

Rib Bone Jack: The Poacher's Path

Rib Bone Jack: The Spareson Spies

Rib Bone Jack: Thief's Honour

Rib Bone Jack: The Devil's Loss

Rib Bone Jack: The Breaking Tide

As ever I dedicate this book to my wife Marie and my children; Samantha, Aidan, Bethany and Megan, who are my constant inspiration for all that I do.

Also, I ask readers to spare a thought for those who have given their lives for their country; not publicly and with great honours being bestowed upon them, but in secret, behind enemy lines, their true sacrifice sometime never being recognised.

The way of things

Still recovering from his wounds, Jack and Camilla have taken up residency at the Spareson house, amongst a bunch of new recruits and a couple of familiar faces.

While Jack awaits his orders from London, a sinister political reshuffle is underway amongst the most powerful and influential men in the country. With the war in Europe once more nearing British shores, the interference of a mysterious group of treacherous aristocrats, casts a dark shadow over preparations for a decisive battle that must surely be on the horizon.

To add irritation to the situation, smuggling has become rife, highlighting how poorly protected the home shores really are. With so much illegal goods coming ashore, the argument is made by the King himself, that Napoleon could walk in just as easily.

Chapter 1

For Stan Gibbs the nightly job of securing the Spareson house was a cherished task; a therapy of types. A spell in a Spanish war prison, culminating in days of torture, had left him mentally and physically scared, yet he was the man the twenty-two new recruits looked to for laughter and amusement; a man who had survived on the back of his own good humour.

"Can we expect the Captain in tonight, Jack?" Gibbs asked as he took the keys from the hook, to lock up for the night.

"Not a chance... While the cat's away!" Jack replied from the chair at the head of the dinning room table, which had always been the focal point of the Spareson house.

"Why the bloody hell doesn't he just get a wife of his own?"

"He's got one somewhere, so he says," Jack replied as he raised himself to his feet to extinguish the lamp in the side room.

"About bloody right, while most of us poor bastards have to go without," Gibbs grumbled, as he made his way out to the stables.

Still limping from the injury that nearly took both his leg and his life, Jack made his way through to the kitchen, where Camilla waited.

"Is it just us?" She asked with the warm smile that had captivated him, almost from the moment they met, on Gatekeeper rock.

"No, Stan's still wandering about."

"And Charlie?"

"The lady!"

"I'm not understanding, you two," she said in her struggling English, seeing the concern on Jack's face for Charlie Halfbasket's antics. "You are friends, but you are not trusting him... It's not nice being not trusted, I know this, more than most."

Jack put his hand on hers, the unspoken gestures still being important between them, even since she had learnt English comparatively well. "I know if Mr Vernance trusts him, it should be fine, but the link to the Lahand family; I just can't put it out of my mind."

"Well you should," she said sternly. "And I know just how," She said, leading him by the hand, up the narrow, twisted staircase, to the room they shared.

The dead of night in the Spareson house was truly silent. A country house with no immediate neighbours; the large, isolated house had been selected for its seclusion, for the purposes of a secret training camp.

With Camilla fast asleep beside him, Jack laid wide awake. Sleeping was often an issue for him. With such ease, his mind would drift back to times and people past, and with enough clarity to feel uncomfortably real.

It was only as he began to drift into a shallow sleep that it happened. The entire house seemed to shake. A simultaneous concoction of deafening noises bombarded his senses. Glass from the small window at the end of the bed sprayed inwards, accompanied by fragments of shattered timber. A mile from the sea, yet the Spareson house was under cannon-fire.

Jack rolled to his right, where Camilla was fumbling for the floor, confused, but clearly unhurt. The room was in total darkness, such was the night. His ears still buzzed from the intensity of the blast, adding to the disarray of his senses.

Eventually he found the door and felt his way to the narrow staircase. Only as he reached the bottom did he see any worthwhile light. "Are you alright, Sir?" Verigan Wilks, one of the new batch of recruits, asked.

"What the bloody hell happened, Wilks?" Jack asked as he stepped into the light from Wilks' lamp.

"The powder shed, Sir!" Three more of the young men gathered behind Wilks, each of them in a similarly confused state.

"Mr Wilks. I want every man accounted for within the next five minutes, and assembled in the dinning room."

"Yes, Sir... What of Captain Halfbasket, Sir?"

"He's not with us tonight," Jack replied as he retrieved his holstered horse pistols from the back of the side room door.

"Mr Gibbs. With me," Jack commanded, upon seeing Gibbs loading a rifle at the back of the room. "Nobody else is to leave the house. Do you understand?"

"Sir," three of them replied half-heartedly.

"Are they so useless?" Gibbs asked, as they hurried onto the rough grass behind the house.

"They make me nervous. Twenty-two strangers, Stan. None of them have been here more than a couple of weeks... Odds are one of them is behind this."

"Shit a brick," Gibbs gasped as he shone his lamp towards the shattered shell of the outbuildings, at the end of the house.

"They used the bloody cannon," Jack said as he looked over the cannon, on the practice deck.

"They could have gone anywhere," Gibbs grumbled, looking into the darkness, in all directions.

"Bring that lamp over here." Jack was kneeling beside the cannon, dabbing the wooden floor of the false ship's deck, with his finger. As the light from Gibbs' lamp cast on the boards, Jack's suspicions were realised. "They came past the pond; two of em," he said as he dabbed his fingers in a thick muddy footprint.

"I preferred the idea of beating a confession out of the youngsters," Gibbs joked in the dry manner that often confused the younger recruits.

"We might still catch up with them," Jack said enthusiastically.

"We'll just break our bloody necks, and we make a pretty good target; the only bloody light for miles."

"The light's blinding you, Stan. I've clobbered a hare and a brace of pheasants on darker nights than this, without so much as a spark of light."

"Officer through and through... Poaching bastard," Stan smirked, knowing he could talk to Jack like that, in the spirit of banter, so long as the recruits weren't in earshot.

"Plod along at you own speed," Jack instructed him as he vanished, limping into the darkness.

"Late night stroll it is then," Gibbs muttered to himself.

Jack hated to admit it, but he still couldn't run at any speed. The break to his leg had been aggravated by the events on the Gatekeeper rock and had taken a frustrating amount of time to heal. The darkness did however give him the edge. He knew there were few paths through the dense bramble ridden woodland, behind the pond and only one of them led to anywhere.

As he joined the pathway, which was generally only used by deer and the occasional hunting party, his eyes became more acclimatised to the lack of light. What had been indistinguishable darkness was now an array of varying shades of black and grey. The few glimmers of light reflecting from leaves and tree trunks, enough to show the way; a complex arrangement of silhouettes presenting the path before him.

The mud under his feet felt sloppy, suggesting the path had been recently walked. He placed a hand on the tree trunks as he progressed along the path, steadying himself as his weak leg began to ache from the pressure. In the distance, a lone dog began to bark, placing in Jack's mind the position of the village, as well as giving a clue to the location of the men.

For a few seconds he lent against a tree, taking the weight off of his right leg. He listened to the few sounds that the night had to offer. The dog was becoming angry; more than just a random bark. The faint sound of a voice in the distance put them at only a hundred yards or so, ahead of him. He drew one of the horse pistols and began to walk forwards; this time at a more gentle pace, allowing himself to continue listening. The voices were getting louder and the dog's bark, more frantic. Ahead of him the trees began to thin and the brambles were replaced by intermittent patches of grass, where livestock grazed from the village.

"If you keep your stupid mouth shut, no bastard will know," a man in a drastically oversized coat snarled as he pushed the second man backwards.

"They heard that bloody bang in London I shouldn't wonder. I'm tellin you, they'll be lookin for us."

"Well they won't bloody well find us if you keep that mouth of yours shut... Else I'll shut it for you ya gutless little shite," the man in the heavy coat snarled, pushing him again. In response the lightly built youngster jumped forwards, grabbing the man in the coat, around the waist.

Jack cocked his pistol, making that unmistakable noise which spoke a thousand words. Both men stood still, absorbing the reality of their situation. "Evening gentlemen," Jack exclaimed, from the darkness. "I'd shoot the pair of you, just for the disturbed sleep, but you're about to explain that, aren't you?"

"It wasn't us, Mr," the younger of the two spluttered, holding his arms just as high in the air as he could reach.

"That is a pity, isn't it Mr Gibbs?"

Gibbs came ambling out from the deer track, bearing the lamp. "That's a tragedy, Sir, but best get to it." Gibbs picked up a length of half rotted rope that laid in the grass, by his feet.

"What the bloody hell are you doing?" the older man demanded, in a state of panic.

"His majesty's property has been damaged. Someone has to hang for it," Jack said in a matter of fact manner. "Get it done, and we can go back to bed. Got to be up in the morning you know; mess to clear up!"

"It was him, Hallman. He arranged it all. A barrel of finest French brandy to shut you lot up, once and for all," the youngster blurted.

"Shut your mouth, you fool," Hallman growled, looking back to the houses behind them. The dog's barking became more insistent and candle-light began to glow in the window of one of the cottages.

"French brandy, it is," said Gibbs, dragging a broken branch from a barrel that nestled in the rough ground at the bottom of the garden. "Treason for sure, Sir."

"Why, because it's French?" Hallman jeered. "There's more French brandy than English ale in these parts, since you and your mates have been pissing about across the water."

"Look, you're just bloody fishermen, I can smell it on you. Tell us who sent you and they can take your place at the end of the rope."

Hallman barred his teeth, snarling, considering his next words.

"I never even saw her. I just came along for half the grog," the younger man insisted, half sobbing in fear.

"Her! It was a bloody woman?" Gibbs said in astonishment.

Jack stared at Hallman. He was looking at his feet, avoiding eye contact with both them and his friend. "If it had been me that arranged it, I'd have wanted the bigger cut."

"It doesn't seem right, a youngster swinging for half a barrel of brandy, especially as it's us that'll be drinking it," Gibbs said, looking over the barrel. "Couldn't we sort this out back at the house, this is going to be bloody heavy; you with your dodgy leg and all."

"Alright, look, we'll tell you all we know," Hallman growled. "She's just a stupid tart that wanted to stop the noise... She turned up in the ale house last night. No bugger had ever seen her before. Just moved in. A widow, so she said."

"What did she look like?" Jack demanded, with all humour struck from his voice.

"She was a beauty. I'm telling you. You would have done the same."

"Let me guess. She offered you some kindnesses if you get it done," Jack said, enthused by the unlikely idea that was going on in his head.

"Thieving bastard," the younger man shouted, prompting more movement in the house behind.

"What did she look like," Jack repeated. "Or would you rather talk about your special payment arrangements in front of your family and neighbours?"

"She was a lady. Dark hair. You wouldn't think it of her. Like royalty, she looked."

As soon as the dawn could provide enough light, Wilks and a couple of the other Spareson recruits watched over the two fishermen, as they cleared up the shattered pieces of the powder shed. "When they've done, beat some bloody sense into them and dump them in the woods, near the village," Jack instructed Gibbs.

"Is this meaning you'll be going to London?" Camilla asked with concern as she sat beside him, on the practice deck.

"No, but that most probably does!" Jack pointed at a rider, through the gap in the trees. A man was approaching the house, sitting so perfectly upright in the saddle, as if on the parade ground, yet dressed in civilian clothes.

"Palace monkey, is it Sir?" Gibbs said dryly.

"A change in fortunes," Jack exclaimed, knowing it would surely represent an end to the long wait for deployment.

Chapter 2

With both hands placed firmly on her buttocks, Father Baker hurriedly pushed Flow onto her horse. "Remember, only Thomas Verance. Don't trust anyone else with it," he stressed, handing her the sealed letter.

"You don't do anything silly while I'm gone, Father," she said with affection, stroking his shoulder like a cherished pet.

"And you don't stop on them roads. Wales is a dangerous place by night," Father Baker warned her with the concern of a jealous lover. He led her horse to the narrow, tree lined track, that ran behind the row of houses, which represented more than half of the tiny village.

"Priest," a robust Welshman's voice called from the road at the front of the cottages. With new urgency, Father Baker hurried Flow away, before making his way along the garden path, at the end of the house. "Priest," the Welshman called again. "It's time to take your whores and go."

"On the say so of whom?" Baker demanded, stepping out from behind the house. The darkness was broken by the flame of four torches, flickering menacingly ahead of him. Within their glow, four men on horseback sat illuminated, but their faces hidden behind leather hoods, implying ill intent.

"In the name of all that's right. God, the church, decency... You shame your sacred vow by dwelling with these sinners."

Baker stepped into the open road, in defiance of their menacing behaviour. They had stopped some thirty yards down the poorly kept road, parading themselves to achieve the optimum terror amongst the women and the priest.

"I've read much of the bible, much about forgiveness, yet all any man talks about is eternal damnation. I'm of a mind to read it differently." As he spoke, the young priest turned his back on the men and walked away from them, towards a small thatched livestock shed, with an open front. Infuriated by his indifference to their threatening display, they began to slowly trot behind him.

"We all know what your interest is, in these tainted souls and it's not right, Sir."

"What would you do for them, Lord Cravith? Flog them, or hang them... It's the easiest thing for a sinner to point out the sins of others."

Enraged by being named, Lord Cravith drew his pistol, but in his angry haste he caused his horse to fidget, making his aim difficult.

"Primed, ready and loaded with nails... Bloody messy way to go!" As he spoke, Baker pulled the sheet from a large ship's cannon, which stood in the little thatched building, trained down the road, directly towards them. In his hand he held a flint and an old file, sufficient to strike a worthy spark.

"What kind of priest are you?" Cravith demanded, taken aback by the weapon.

"What brings you out at night, Sir? I know it's nothing to do with these women." He gestured towards the row of cottages, which were now illuminated. In three of the upstairs windows the silhouettes of women pointing muskets could be clearly seen, further enraging Cravith. One of his companions turned his horse anxiously, before moving close to Cravith and whispering close to his ear.

"Take the time you have, to return these harlots back to the London streets, where you found them," Cravith warned as he studied the most unnatural sight of the three women, reputedly of loose morals, pointing muskets directly at him. "Whatever's going on here, it isn't right," he huffed as he turned his horse about and rode into the darkness.

Chapter 3

Jack had found an ale house that suited his tastes
perfectly, upon his return from Spain. It was constantly
rowdy, with two back rooms for gambling and a wide
range of other pursuits, which, for one reason or another,
were better practised with some privacy. It wasn't that he
was so keen on the various illicit pursuits of the ale house,
it was just an atmosphere he loved. He also found that in
that particular ale house, he could achieve a level of
anonymity that his colourful reputation would seldom
allow. It went by the name of 'The King's Tavern' and sat
on a murky back street, which matched it's character
perfectly, playing host to dodgy street traders and
whoring establishments.

When he set off from the Spareson house, Jack had
warned Camilla that he may be a few days, knowing that
at long last Thomas Verance had a purpose for him. As the
two embraced at the front of the Spareson house, Jack
had told her of the little old couple that ran the guest
house near the palace, and how he'd be sure to get a
good night's sleep there, before his meeting with
Verance, the next day. He didn't make a habit of lying to
her, and he certainly didn't plan to be cheating with some
pox ridden street whore, he just knew her more prudish
upbringing wouldn't allow her to understand his choice of
accommodation.

The ride to London had been unpleasant. A persistent
heavy rain had set in for the day, making the giant log fire
at the back of the King's tavern all the more welcome. He

sat alone, cradling a jug of ale as the evening passed. Amid the drunkenness, there were few words to be heard. Shouting, jeering and singing all seemed to merge into one confusing noise, yet this was to Jack, pure entertainment. Goods were being traded openly. Boxes with the writing scraped off of them, confirming their illicit content, were hauled across the large crowded room, to a chubby man, in a straw hat, who had set up shop in the darkened corner of the room.

Throughout the evening Jack kept the same spot, by the fire. He laughed along with the banter and cheered as a drunken whore lost her clothes to a bet, but in his mind there was a hint of sadness. He remembered Peter Scoulter's love of such places and considered just how much more rowdy that tavern would have been, if Peter had been there. He then thought of the Bone house, back home; his very own ale house, purchased with French gold. He hadn't said as much, not to anyone, but he felt exiled from it. To take Camilla home would open a can of worms like no other. In a county were neighbouring villages were treated as foreigners, a Spanish woman would be seen as a public enemy, most particularly by his own family.

It was only as the evening broke down into a series of drunken brawls that Jack decided to retreat to his room. He felt like a magnet for trouble, inevitably finding himself in the thick of every scrape and skirmish that came his way, often generated by his own notoriety. This was something he knew he needed to avoid, if he was to continue in the service of the crown.

The next morning, the approach to the previously low key residence of Thomas Verance, on the edge of the palace grounds, had an almost chilling air to it. There was a heavy presence of soldiers; far more than the usual guard. As he got close, he noticed two smartly dressed men, apparently in charge of something, enough that they were giving orders to the soldiers.

"State your business, Sir," one of the regular palace guards demanded, long before he reached the pedestrian gate, which was normally only guarded by one man.

"Its Jack Bones, Harrup. You've seen me before. Three times, if not more."

"Yes, Sir. I still have to see your papers, with all of this, Sir."

Jack produced from his pocket the letter from Thomas Verance, just enough to display it's broken seal. "What is going on, Harrup?"

"A killing, Sir. Smithy, the door guard, cut from ear to ear, so they reckon. People saying they were after, you know who!"

"Is he safe?" Jack asked anxiously, looking around Harrup with increased concern.

"Yes, Sir. The man's the luck of the devil, the one night he was on business, it was."

Jack smiled politely. "May I?" he said, being keen to have a proper look.

"Oh, yes, of course, Sir," Harrup said, at last stepping aside.

Jack made his way towards the little cottage, which had become both residence and centre of operations to Thomas Verance; the King's spymaster. "Where's that wretched stable boy," he heard Verance demand, as he walked over, doing his best to disguise his limp.

"There are other servants, Sir," one of the well dressed civilians suggested, patronisingly.

"I do realise that, damn you, man," Verance snapped loudly, enough to attract the attention every other man present. "Jack," he exclaimed with relief. "Tell this damned fool why it has to be the stable boy."

"The stable boy is a simpleton, Sir. Mr Verance hired him for the purpose, because he knew he couldn't read a word."

"And I have papers spread all over the floor... I've told you before, nobody touches them but the stable boy."

"Yes, Sir," the man said, turning to the path behind him, looking anxiously for the stable boy.

"Do they have much?" Jack asked as he pushed his wheelchair towards the corpse of the guard, knowing there were documents in Mr Verance's possession that could alter the entire war and cost many lives in the process.

"No. Everything of state importance is under lock and key, but I still don't want those scoundrels pawing over my private correspondence."

"What went on, then? What were they after?"

"It was clearly an organised gang, Mr Verance," the other overdressed civilian interrupted. "The rogue was found with his breachers disarranged... I have men asking around the local harlots. One of them was surely hired to act as a distraction, while the gang attacked."

Jack dropped down onto his good knee, gritting his teeth against the pain such actions still caused to his right leg. With little care, he lifted the dead guards head by the hair, exposing a single clean cut to the throat. "Cold. Without hesitation... I've met many killers, but few kill this easily," Jack said quietly, engrossed in his own thoughts.

"May I ask who I'm addressing, young man?"

"This is Lieutenant Bones," Verance explained. "And this is Simon Brockstone; a man with some skill in these matters."

Brockstone raised his eyebrow, deliberately highlighting his knowledge of Jack's chequered reputation. "Sir, with all due respect, matters such as these should be handled in the correct manner."

Verance didn't reply. He just glanced at Jack, waiting for his response. "Mr Brockstone is of course right," Jack said with a smirk. "But I would like to present myself as an expert witness."

"Expert in what, young Sir?"

"Killing, Mr Brockstone," Jack said, fixing a chilling stare upon the pompous investigator.

"Very well. What do you have to add to my investigation?"

"There was only one attacker. A woman," Jack began, once more struggling to hold back a smirk.

"Ridiculous. No woman could over power a trained soldier," Brockstone interrupted dismissively.

"Trained soldier; my foot. Palace guards are known by every other regiment as King's housemaids," Jack said abruptly. "And this man wasn't exactly battle ready." He pointed to his loosened belt and partially fitted breachers, to prove his point.

"Men were seen acting suspiciously in the street. We are looking for three men in their twenties, dressed in labourer's clothes," Brockstone argued insistently, offended that a youngster of ill repute was questioning his judgement.

"There are many thousands of young men, acting suspiciously in this town," Jack replied calmly. "Most of them will be dressed in labourer's clothes, due to them being labourer's." Jack stood back up and walked to the one small window, which had been broken to gain access. "It's a dainty labourer that got through that, don't you think... If there were three men, would the first man in not have opened the bigger window, for his friends?"

"Speculation, Sir," Brockstone grumbled, looking over the larger window, which had been untouched.

Jack took from the broken glass, on the edge of the window, three threads of fine cotton. He presented them to Thomas Verance. "Fine cloth, from a petticoat."

"It could be anything," but as he spoke, Brockstone's eye was drawn by a depression in a mole hill, directly under the window. It wasn't much, but it was clearly a partial bare footprint.

"She would have kicked off her shoes and dress, there," Jack commented with a sense of victory. "Her name is Elaina Crass; a high ranking Spanish spy."

"How do you know that," Verance asked scornfully, convinced that he had taken the argument too far.

"It was her that organised the attack on the Spareson house, night before last. The men identified her, Sir... If you press your witnesses, you'll find she paid them to make a false statement." Brockstone looked back at him, this time not speaking. He looked worried. More than just the embarrassment of having been shown up by someone he considered in every way inferior to himself. "You did get names and addresses? Just in case she were to return!"

"You must understand, Sir, there was a lot going on. An attack on the palace grounds, Sir. So much focus on the immediate security, there just wasn't time for such details." Brockstone was pleading directly to Thomas Verance, in effect begging for his esteemed position and reputation.

"I'm sure you've done your best, Mr Brockstone, but it would appear we have identified the perpetrator," Verance replied politely, but with no attempt to spare his embarrassment. "Now if you'll excuse me, I have matters to discuss with the Lieutenant."

"Sir. I must warn you of the dangers of consorting with such a disreputable individual," Brockstone called desperately, as Jack wheeled his chair towards the gardens.

Verance glanced back. "I should warn you against insulting such a disreputable individual," his manner bordering on a threat.

"I never was much for gardening; never had the time for it. Now it's all that keeps me sane," Verance began, just for the purposes of light conversation, until they were safely out of earshot. "Of course, legs would be a bonus for my new hobby, but I have servants to do the donkey work, so I mustn't complain." The ever present sorrow in his scarred face told a less cheerful story, and the small plot he had been permitted by the palace, concealed behind a tall hedge, confirmed the stories that he had been hidden from view, in fear of scaring the royal children and guests.

"It's a fine hobby, Sir," Jack replied obligingly.

"It is what it is!" Verance bashed a rose bush with a short cane, emphasising his frustration at what his life had become. "What of the Spareson house, what happened there?"

"We lost a few windows and a shed full of powder, and gained a barrel of brandy, but it was Elaina, right enough. She was in London by the time they blew the shed. It was just a distraction."

"I'm inclined to agree," Verance said, considering his next words carefully. "They've done for Mr Weaverton. He's due to hang."

"He's the bloody provost marshal. I thought he was beyond the law," Jack said in amazement.

"Found guilty on the testimony of Sederic Fraser; one of the few truly honest men in this country."

"Guilty of what?" Jack asked with an air of disbelief.

"Dishonest conduct. Taking bribes and the like."

"Sir. That man guarded a boat full of gold with his life and didn't take so much as a bootlace that didn't belong to him."

Verance nodded. "Both honest men. I agree." He pointed to a small tuft of grass at the base of a rose bush, with his cane. "Would you mind, Jack. They grow so fast."

While jack carefully pulled the weed, avoiding the rose thorns, Verance once more considered his words. "Yesterday I gave a rear admiral a pistol and told him to do the honourable thing... The Major wouldn't have been so merciful, but my ways aren't without their benefits!"

"He told you something?"

"He made good his wrong before he went... Charlie Halfbasket and three Sparesons visited his house before the news got out. The butler and the cook were shot on sight."

"French or Spanish?"

"Too dead to tell us, but they were killers through and through. The real servants were found, salted in barrels, in the cellar."

Jack winced at the picture in his head. "Are you sure about Halfbasket?" he asked sheepishly, having already taken the matter up with him, when he first learnt of Charlie's connection to the Lahand family.

"Captain Halfbasket has proven his loyalty beyond doubt. I recommended him to the Major myself and I stand by the fact that he's the best of us." Verance was, as Jack expected, angered by Jack's doubts, but his savage response reflected just how much trust had been bestowed on the Captain and how much damage a traitor could do, in his position. "All you need to know about is your mission; you and Mr Dewson."

"I'll be glad to have Horry and that rifle by my side," Jack said enthusiastically.

"This isn't bloody Spain," Verance snapped back, his anger still not quelled. "You're to watch and listen, without killing anyone."

"Where are we going, Sir?"

"South Wales; the back door to England, and according to my man there, it's wide open... You are to replace a revenue man that died there last week. Mr Dewson will be joining a priest in one of the villages. Things have been getting a bit sticky of late."

"Bart Baker?"

"Who else?" Verance replied, at last mellowing his tone. "The smugglers along that coast line could bring in the entire bloody French army and we wouldn't notice. We need to bring them to heel, Jack."

Chapter 4

"It's a beautiful land, Jack Sir?" Horry Dewson commented, in awe of the breath-taking hillside ahead of him, as they rode into Wales.

"Too bloody hilly for my liking," Jack complained as another steep, winding road presented itself. "If we were looking for sheep smugglers I'd understand it."

"Don't seem right, somehow; playing tax man," Dewson grumbled yet again, it being an issue he had complained about throughout the journey.

"You know by now there's more to it than that. Regardless, we might get a swig of French Brandy out of the deal," Jack said with a grin.

"Sack of salt, more like. That's our luck," Dewson grumbled as they approached a fork in the road.

"Good luck horry. I hope to find you in a couple of days." Jack reached across and shook Dewson by the hand as the equal that he had always treated him.

Their destinations were only five miles apart, but they quite deliberately took different routes to get there, even though the same road would have been the sensible option for both places. If a link between the two were to be established by the locals, both their missions could have been in jeopardy.

Jack continued along the better kept road, towards Tenby, meeting the occasional traveller along the way, but more than anything, he met drovers, driving sheep and cattle. This was the main trade of the area. The idea that there was some vast network of smugglers and distributors operating amongst such simple folk, seemed unlikely.

He watched as a whole family drove four pigs past him; the pigs washed and brushed for market, but the people affording themselves no such luxuries. The children stared as he past, their eyes shining against their filthy skin, while the father spoke a single word in Welsh, which Jack assumed to be an obligatory greeting.

As he continued, he was absorbed by his thoughts. 'How was he to catch smugglers if he was assigned to the revenue?' It made no sense. As a dock worker or a fisherman he would soon find a way into trusted circles, but the revenue; they were marked men. His orders were to openly investigate the death of Bryn Davies; the young revenue officer, found floating in the harbour with his head smashed in. 'Why was this an issue that should be seen as important to Thomas Verance?' It had become a habit to question the realities behind his orders, never taking a word at face value.

Upon the sight of a labourer, walking his way, he decided he was only going to get that one chance to look around as anything other than a marked man. "Afternoon," he said as he drew his horse level with the man on foot.

"Sir," the man replied cautiously. Despite the fact he had selected clothes befitting those of a respectable man of modest means, Jack still had a hawkish way about him; a look that put a man on edge.

"Would you know if there's somewhere that sells anything more than the horse piss this wretched country has offered me so far?" Jack spoke with deliberate provocation. He never trusted overly agreeable people himself and considered with his horse pistols under his jacket, there was no fight he couldn't handle.

"That'll be the other side of the border. Land of piss. In these parts we eat and drink like Kings." The man spoke bluntly but not out of turn, noticing the handle of one of the pistols protruding from his jacket. "Are you buying or selling?"

"Is there a market?" Jack asked, looking the man in the eyes as if he was trying to read his mind.

"Them matters are taken care of around here, but there's brandy and finest Irish whisky in The Three Oaks, just over the next hill, and plenty else if a man's of a mind."

"Much obliged to you, Sir," Jack said as he moved his horse off, already considering his strategy.

The Three Oaks stood back from the road, marked only by three crudely drawn trees on a board, nailed to the front of what appeared to be, in all other respects, a rural cottage.

He tied his horse to a cart, with a broken wheel, which had clearly stood in the yard for some time. He took a while about it, just to give himself time to look over his surroundings. Apart from two goats tethered at the front, the place initially appeared empty. As he approached the door he half expected to find it locked, such was it's sleepy character; yet the door opened.

He descended a single step into a room of crudely fashioned tables and a sawdust floor, similar to some of the fisherman's pubs he had known, back in Norfolk.

Of the three men in the room, two labourers, in their twenties looked up from their ale, just staring, as if a stranger was something so unusual, despite the fact the pub sat on the main road. The third considerably older man, didn't move. He remained slumped over his ale jug, giving little reason to think he was conscious.

Jack walked over to the bar, which consisted of a wooden bench wedged across the corner of the room, blocking the doorway to the back room. He looked for a minute, not calling for service. The room at the back was narrow; a cross between a kitchen and a barrel store, stacked to such a degree that there appeared little room for any kind of food preparation.

"Hello, soldier!" came a strong Welsh woman's voice from the main doorway. "You useless old shite, could have served the young gentleman," she snapped in a contrasting tone, swiping the older man around the back of the head, yet still not prompting him to make any serious movement. The woman was well in her fifties and quite round; both in the body and face, with glowing red cheeks that drew the eye to her jolly face. "We get a lot of your kind around here, and you're very welcome."

"What is my kind?" Jack asked as she seemed to glide under the bar table, in a manner you might expect of a woman half her size.

"I watched you walk in. Wounded out of the army, but still clinging to the gun," she smiled, demonstrating her few remaining yellow and black teeth. "The only use they'll be to you is if you can dig a ditch with them." She was pointing to the two pistol handles protruding from his jacket, which Jack had deliberately displayed for the purposes of strategy.

"Very good," Jack smiled obligingly. "I've had my fill of weak ale of late. Do you have brandy?"

"Do you have the money to pay for what I have to give?" she asked, her eyes twinkling with joy. "The army don't leave you boys with much when they've done with you!"

Jack looked back at her and smiled, but didn't immediately speak. He considered his response carefully. "I'm not short," he eventually replied, looking back to see the two younger men still unashamedly staring. "Question is, do you?.. My brother has a boat. We're running it from Ireland, just started."

Every bit of joy disappeared from the landlady's face. "Trouble with you soldier boys, you think you're indestructible. You'll be dead by the end of the week. Bloody fool."

"Who's going to do that then?" he asked smugly.

"Boy, if you don't know I'm not going to tell you, but I will tell you that we've a system in these parts, and there are those that don't like it if the system gets messed with."

Jack smiled as if he fully understood what she was talking about. "And what if I wanted to join this system. Who would I talk too?"

"They'll be talking to you, soon enough," she said with a cautionary tone, before turning to fill an ale jug for the old man at the table. "Take that across to him and come under. Have some of what I have to offer. She lifted her dress slightly, just to confirm what it was she was selling. "It's a damned sight cheaper than a night of drinking and you won't fall off your horse when you've had your fill."

Jack looked at her, struggling to hide his disgust as a picture formed in his head. He glanced back through the open door behind her, considering just how much he wanted to know the nature and origin of the goods stored there. "Everyone comes under in the end," She smiled, pointing under the table. "So long as he's a jug of ale in front of him, he's happy with it."

"Then I best deliver it to him," Jack said cheerfully before placing the ale jug next to the now entirely unconscious landlord.

As he ducked down, under the bar, he met a pair of puffed up, reddened ankles, protruding from beneath her dress; a reflection of the rest of her body, he assumed. As she led him through to the back room, he pictured in his mind Camilla's perfect body, waiting for him, back at the Spareson house.

"Give us a hand with these damned laces, will you lovie?" she said, trying and failing to drag the dress over her head, briefly exposing an over sized irregularly shaped rump. "New dress you see. Not made for getting out of...

I'm lucky I always have keen helpers." Jack ignored her, instead looking over the stacks of goods. As well as the barrels, there was tobacco and an open keg, full of pepper, all roughly stacked with no interest in hiding it.

"French brandy," Jack exclaimed with delight at the sight of a barrel partially covered by a bale of wool.

"I bet your brother can't get that," she huffed, struggling to loosen the dress, which was draped partially over her head. "Now be a lovie and help me with this bloody dress."

"Too much woman for me!" Jack said loudly, with an air of relief as he bolted under the bar and across the public room, towards the door.

Chapter 5

By the time Jack reached Tenby, it was entirely dark, with an autumn chill blowing off the sea. He assumed the customs house would be closed for the night, yet as he walked to the corner of the back street, off the harbour, lamplight glowed in the window of the stern, uninviting looking building. 'No time like the present,' he thought, deciding to knock on the door, on the off chance.

He waited, slightly nervously as a chair scraped across the floor, inside. Gentle footsteps paced towards the door at a slow, unhurried pace, suggesting to Jack that callers at such an hour weren't unusual. The door slowly opened, revealing a tall, well dressed man in his forties.

"Jack Spoons, Sir. I'm to report here for duty, Sir." He spluttered obligingly, keen to give the impression of a man of lowly rank.

"Mr Spoons," the man said with surprise. "We weren't expecting you for a couple of days yet... Do come in."

"You work late, Sir," Jack commented, seeing the open ledger on the desk.

"Everything has to be logged. It's not just about chasing smugglers around the countryside you know."

"Are you Mr Winter, Sir?"

"Oh yes, where's my manners. Leonard Winter," he replied, extending his hand. "It's been a long day. We deal with the honest men by day, who just want to pay what's owed, and chase the dishonest ones by night."

Jack gladly shook his hand, taking the opportunity to study the man by the dim lamplight. He certainly looked in need of sleep. His eyes were hooded, as if it was a constant effort to keep them open, but more than that, he looked troubled.

"I trust my role will involve chasing the dishonest? I have little experience of honest men," Jack joked, raising a half-hearted smile, in an attempt to lighten the mood.

"I'm told your first task is to investigate the death of young Davies," winter said, without cracking a smile.

"Yes, Sir."

"Then I can assume London have sent you to keep an eye on us," he said sternly, sliding the ledger on the table towards Jack. "You'll find the passage out the back leads to the pound; everything seized is in there and in the ledger and everything that leaves is also logged."

"Sir, the only requirement made of me is that I investigate and report on the death. After that, I am at your disposal."

"Think yourself a bit of a thief catcher, do you?" Winter said in an only slightly softer tone. He picked up a bat from the side of his desk and pushed aside the lapel of Jack's coat, to expose one of the pistols. "That's how men get killed. If we start shooting at them, they'll shoot back... You only use them wretched things if I specifically say so. Do you understand?"

"Yes, Sir!"

"Wounded out of the army?" Winter pointed his bat to Jack's right leg, which he had immediately noticed to be lame.

"Yes, Sir," Jack agreed. It seemed to be an assumption people made, since he gained the limp and it made his story that bit more plausible, so he thought he may just as well go with it.

"What regiment?"

"Palace guard, Sir... It's how I got this job, Sir. Not what you know but who you know."

"Quite so," he agreed with a wry glance. "Not front line fighting then?" He once more pointed to Jack's leg.

"Fell off my horse, Sir."

At last Winter smiled. "You'll spend more time on a boat than a horse. I don't recommend you fall off that either, though." He turned, moving towards the tiny stove, which both heated the room and kept the kettle hot. "I'd offer you a drink, but I've almost lost the fire."

"Thank you, Sir, but I must present myself to my lodgings at a reasonable hour," Jack replied, sensing that the conversation was close to an end. "Would it be possible to see what is known of the man's death, in the morning, Sir?"

"Oh, do forgive me. I assumed you knew. We have two young men for that. Looks like young Davies tried to apprehend them on his own... A lesson to us all."

"Smugglers?"

"Of course. Running whiskey from Ireland; our biggest problem. Some of them go across in little more than a bath tub! Drowning does for a few of them. We get the rest, sooner or later."

"Would it be possible to speak to them? Just for my report," Jack asked, as much as anything, to get an understanding of what was being smuggled, from an independent source.

"You'll have to be quick. They hang in the morning; eight o'clock sharp, on the heath."

"Then I may have to report in late, Sir, if that's agreeable to you?"

"Oh, we'll be there. It's us doing the hanging," Winter said with hint of pride in his voice.

The notion took Jack aback. "Is that to be part of my duties?" Jack asked with blatant concern.

"Certainly not. My people do like to be part of the whole process though, from start to finish as it were, and it does seem to instil a certain respect in the locals, otherwise they'd laugh at us."

Jack smiled back unconvincingly, failing to hide his discomfort with Winter's methods. "I must be finding my lodgings, Sir. I will see you in the morning."

"Bright and early Mr Spoons!"

As Jack left the building, Winter slid the two large bolts across, anxiously looking back down the corridor behind him, which led to the impounded goods. He waited at the door for half a minute or more, just listening for Jack's footsteps as he walked away.

"It's not safe for either of us, you coming here," Winter insisted, staring into the darkness of the passageway. He had the look of a frightened rabbit about him; a mix of anger that he was being put in a dangerous position and raw fear of the man.

"Was that him," Halls asked bluntly, as he stepped out from the darkness.

"It was, and he's already asking questions."

"About the Davies boy?"

"Of course. What else?" Winter snapped. "It was too much; killing him. He could have been bought off."

"Killing off is cheaper!" Halls replied dismissively, being keen to intimidate Winter with every word. "Anyway, the boy was always going to talk, you said that yourself."

"I'll tell you now, we can't hide another killing amongst our own, least of all, one from London." Winter made his way to his desk, nervously avoiding eye contact with Halls. "We do it my way in future, otherwise we'll have soldiers on the streets within weeks."

"Can he be bought?" Halls gestured to the door, where Jack had just left.

"I would expect so. He's just a youngster. Can't even stay on his horse. His leg's been broken."

Halls raised his eyebrows, suddenly interested in what Winter had to tell him. "A pair of pistols and an accent?"

Winter nodded. "Do you know him?"

"I don't know. There is a lad... If it is him, London are on to us." Halls had changed his tone. He was faced with a mix of emotions. The chance to settle an old score was on one hand to be welcomed, but he knew full well there was a good chance such a confrontation may not go his way.

Chapter 6

It was well before eight when Jack got to the heath, where a tight crowd had already gathered around Lucifer's tree; the name the locals had given the crude gallows, which stood, permanently as a warning to would be wrong doers.

He hurried his pace as he heard the gasps, boos and cheers of the crowd; a tell tale sign that a man had been hung. By the time he had got to the gathering, the young man's foot was giving its last twitches; his rag like body hanging otherwise motionless.

Behind the crowd he could see a cage, in a cart, guarded by a full bearded man, who resembled in every way, a fisherman. As quickly as his lame leg would carry him, Jack hurried to the cart. He knew, with luck he would have a couple of minutes to talk to the other brother, if he was of a mind.

As he approached the cart, a young man armed with a wooden bat, remarkably like the one he had seen Winter with, the night before, stepped forwards. "Nobody is to approach the prisoner," he growled, holding the bat forwards.

"I'm with the revenue. I have Mr Winter's approval to talk with the prisoner."

"I am the bloody revenue. You're nothing to do with us." he pushed the bat towards Jack's face as he spoke, only falling short by a few inches.

Jack didn't speak. He just stared back; not so much as blinking as he wrapped his left arm in a circular motion, around the bat, twisting it from the man's hand. "Take it up with Winter," Jack snarled, pushing past him with contempt.

With the first brother dead, the crowd seemed to focus on the activity around the cage as the older revenue man trained his musket on him. Jack ignored both the crowd and the musket. The second prisoner sat, sobbing into his hands, hiding his eyes from the sight of his hanging brother.

"I can't offer you much, but I'd hear the truth from you, if you were of a mind to give it," Jack said loudly enough to make his intention clear to anyone close.

"Youngest brother," the young man snivelled, pointing in the direction of the gallows, whilst still covering his eyes with the other hand. "I've told you people what you want to hear. What bloody more do you want?"

Jack considered the story of the Rear Admiral as two armed men pushed their way through the crowd. A condemned man would gladly confess to somebody else's crimes if it kept their family safe. A confession extracted from a man who was going to hang for smuggling anyway was worthless.

"What is it you think we wanted to hear?" Jack asked, as the two guards opened the cage.

"We only asked for one thing; to hang together, but you bastards couldn't do that, could you. Couldn't spare an extra bit of rope, so I didn't have to see that." The young man at last uncovered his eyes as he was dragged from the cart; fear and horror being overtaken by anger.

"Which one of you killed the revenue man?" Jack demanded as the young man was dragged through the crowd. To his frustration, the older, bearded revenue man stepped in front of him, preventing him from following.

"Can't you let a man hang in piece, bloody boy?" the old man growled through the forest of greying facial hair. Jack turned and kicked the earth in frustration as the crowd closed up in front of him, cheering and goading to such an extent that another word was unlikely to be heard from the youngster.

He walked over to the cart and pressed his head against the bars, considering his next move. The young man had told him nothing of substance, yet he felt there was so much more that could have been told. He climbed awkwardly onto the cart; his weak leg making such actions difficult. He was of a mind to thinking that if nobody was going to tell him anything, there actions just might.

Looking across the crowd, he saw a sea of spectators, each of them gathered for there own macabre amusement, but more than that, as a stranger looking in, he could see everyone else as well. A family gathered at the front, screaming and sobbing as the customs officers stood the terrified young man beneath the very basic gibbard.

Jack studied the men doing the hanging. There were a couple of watchmen who seemed to be restricting their participation to that of crowd control, but those operating the noose were customs men; Winter commanding their every move.

It horrified Jack to see the method of hanging used. A rope was draped over the gibbard and the noose slipped around the man's neck. He was given no opportunity to speak as was tradition in England, those of a religious disposition believing it important for a man to be given the chance to repent.

The moment the rope was around his neck, two men hoisted the rope, dragging him from his feet, allowing him to dangle, kicking the last vestiges of life from his body. It was the cruellest thing. There was no hope of his neck breaking, bringing an early end to his suffering, just slow choking misery. What seemed worse to Jack was the fact that the crowd didn't protest; not one of them. His conclusion was that this must surely be their usual practice, rather than an extra cruelty to a man who had killed one of their own.

He lowered himself back down from the cart, determined to confront Winter as to why the hangings had been conducted earlier than he had told him. His anger at the whole sorry spectacle demanded that he confront the man, but as he forced his way through the crowd, he considered the wider picture. Just what was he going to learn by publicly challenging the man in charge. No truths were going to be told, but there was also a risk that such a challenge would induce a wall of silence, crippling his investigation.

"Good morning Mr Winter," Jack exclaimed as he eventually reached the front, having had to wrestle his way past such a crowd of rabidly excited onlookers.

"Mr Spoons. Glad you could join us," Winter replied pushing at the pair of at last motionless legs, which dangled by his head. "Give him another minute, just to be sure," he ordered his men, before approaching Jack. "Sorry we were a little early, but we had a pair to do."

"I hadn't noticed," Jack replied with an obliging smile. "I got what I needed, anyway."

"What's that then?" Winter asked, suspecting Jack had something on him.

"A confession! What else?" Jack said with a surprised and almost accusing tone. "I will of course make my findings known to my superiors in London." He had selected his best pompous, self important manner to speak to Winter, he considered it to be a language he would understand.

"I do have one concern, Mr Winter," Jack stressed, his face full of false concern.

"Go on," Winter said, preoccupied as two of his men lowered the body down for the family to take.

"It's the lack of a Vicar or a Priest. Someone to ease the soul into the afterlife." They could have been the words of Bart Baker. Words he had undoubtedly heard him speak in the past; now used for Jack's own ends.

"The local Vicar refused. He says such souls are lost."

"Yet that's not surely the teachings of the church. Are we not all Gods children?"

"Of course, but some more than others," Winter replied with a smile.

"I would quite like to get to know the local area. Have a ride around some of the villages, keeping a watchful eye for smugglers, of course... If I were to stumble across a priest, who would be prepared to take on such a task, would I be at liberty to arrange something?"

"I can see how a village vicar might be glad of the work," Winter agreed. "However, if you are planning a sight seeing tour, I must insist you take a guide. What would London think if you had an accident... There's many more rocks around here than in London for a horse to stumble on, you know." Winter pointed at Jack's leg and grinned as he spoke, taking the opportunity to highlight what he saw as his vulnerability.

"Mr March," Winter called through the rapidly dispersing crowd, beckoning for him to come over. The young man with the bat stepped forwards, looking concerned that he was to be chastised, either for not stopping Jack, or for trying to stop him. "Mr March. This is our new man from London. Jack Spoons," Winter said, formally introducing Jack. "This is Glyn March. He'll see you are properly taken care of, during your time with us."

March smiled slightly and nodded, as if they hadn't already met. His eyes seemed to glisten with joy as he looked on Jack, as if to promise mischief. "Mr Spoons is keen to take a tour of our parish, Glyn. Perhaps you'd care to take him on some house calls."

March looked at Jack with contempt. "Is it right, Sir. Is he the new man?"

"From London, no less." Winter's eyes fixed on March, as if to convey caution; a signal Jack immediately noticed. "Perhaps some of the inland villages."

Chapter 7

Words were few between Jack and Glyn March. An air of mutual loathing and distrust existed between them, forged the very moment they had met.

"Where are we going first, Mr March," Jack eventually asked as March led him inland, along a road that quickly turned to no more than a poorly kept and seldom used herder's track.

"Inland," March replied abruptly, not breaking his focus from the road ahead.

"It's a beautiful land you have," Jack said, again attempting conversation, if only for the purposes of gaining information.

"Don't grow shit!" March grunted, still with eyes unnaturally fixed to the road ahead. His determination not to talk was only compromised by his curiosity. "Tell me then, if you want to talk. Where'd you get the pistols? My guess is mummy bought you them to stop the nasty bad men getting you, and if you ever did pull them, you'd blow your bloody feet off!"

"Sounds like you've got me worked out," Jack said with a weak smile, imitating the person March assumed him to be.

"The problem is, Mr Halls isn't so sure," March spoke with a guarded tone, as if he was testing Jack's reaction.

"Should I know Mr Halls? Is he with the revenue?"

"What he says, goes. Know that and you'll be fine." March once more fixed his vision on the road ahead; not just to avoid eye contact, as before, but to identify the two men, waiting on horseback at the fork in the road.

It looked so much like a trap, yet it came with the promise of information. The name Halls wasn't one that he had been briefed on, but then, as ever, the information from Verance was sketchy, at best.

As they neared the two men, March began speaking in Welsh, to which they replied in the same tongue. Both men seemed to be studying him, as if he was the focus of the conversation.

Jack's horse began to fidget; something it had done throughout the morning. "You really can't control a bloody horse, can you," March said without a hint of amusement, as they rode past the two men.

"Saddle's playing her up," Jack replied vaguely, blatantly studying the two men as he rode past them. Each of them had a shortened cart wheel spoke with a leather wrist strap, hanging on their saddle. Different to the purposefully fashioned clubs he had seen the revenue carry. They were dressed in heavy coats; the sort of thing he associated with fishermen. They stared out from beneath the over-sized coats like crows, trying to gage if a dying animal was dead enough to eat. Jack purposefully looked them in the eyes and nodded, as if they were just passing travellers.

No sooner was he passed them than a figure on horseback appeared in the open ground, a hundred yards or so, ahead. He was different. He sat proudly and upright. His clothes were that of a gentleman, though practical, for the purposes of riding such rough ground as the Welsh hills had to offer. He was in his fifties, but didn't carry the excess weight that Jack associated with retired army officers. None the less, that is what he assumed him to be.

"You're a long way from Norfolk," the man called, in good spirit, as Jack approached. Jack focused his gaze on the man all the more, guessing they had met before.

"Yes, Sir," Jack replied, assuming him to be one of the countless officers he had met in his past dealings. "I don't seem to be able to place your face."

"It is our mutual misfortune that we have not yet been formally introduced, but we know each other well." Jack was now only six feet from him, studying his face all the harder for the cryptic statement. "If we're going by assumed names, and you are Jack Spoons, I am Elm Halls." He squinted as he spoke his name, studying Jack's reaction.

Jack reached for his pistol as a reflex reaction, but stopped just as quickly to the sound of the hammer of March's pistol. "Elmshall," Jack exclaimed, glaring back with the hatred he carried for the cold blooded woman murderer.

"The very same... Bones. Spoons. If you'd been a little more imaginative with your choice of name, I might not have worked it out."

"But then we might not have had this introduction," Jack said with unimpressed sarcasm.

Elmshall smiled back politely, as if it was a society function. "I heard of young Scoulter's misfortune."

"From the woman that killed him, no doubt... It is you that's been bringing her and her friends into the country, isn't it?"

"You're a bright one, for a turd shoveller," Elmshall said, breaking eye contact for a moment to locate the position of the other two men. Jack pushed his knee hard into the saddle, just to make his mare fidget enough to see the men in his peripheral vision.

"So it's all come down to money... Booze, people; anything to line your your stinking pocket."

"I'm not short of money. It's somewhere to spend it that I lack... Thanks to you and your friends, I'm not welcome in England, and the French hold me personally responsible for their losses on Yarmouth beach... It was only when I offered them England's back door key that they wanted to know me again."

"And the Spanish too?"

"Of course. I find the climate agreeable!" Elmshall looked across again to the two men, who were now about fifty yards away. He reached inside his jacket, and produced a leather purse. "Mr March, I've already explained the rules of the game to the others. There's about two years worth of revenue man's wages in there. It will be split between the survivors."

"Survivors?" March said with a grin.

"Two pistols. Three men. Fair odds if the stories I've heard are true," Elmshall said, looking back at Jack. "For the purposes of sport, I won't be shooting. You have my word on that."

"You may as well just hand me the purse, now," Jack said, pulling his coat back from his pistols.

"Shoot him, Mr March," Elmshall ordered.

As the first word passed Elmshall's lips, Jack slid from his saddle, putting the flank of his horse between him and March. As he moved, he pulled from beneath the saddle his heavy bladed knife. It was one perfectly coordinated movement, that could have gone so easily wrong, but before March could fire a shot, Jack's knife wedged into his throat, removing him from his saddle; dead.

As Elmshall trotted from the field of battle, Jack pulled his mare around, shielding himself from the pistol shots of the other two riders. Both men were now close; riding hard, each pointing a pistol, searching for a clear shot. Jack drew one of his pistols. Now, in his own mind at least, he had the advantage.

The thundering of the hooves seemed amplified as a decisive drum beat, but experience had taught him to shut that out. With adrenaline in charge, he released the rein, to avoid the pulling of the spooked horse, shaking his hand. In one smooth action he pointed and shot the first man from his saddle, before dropping that pistol and drawing the second. In that couple of seconds, the remaining rider rode in close, attempting to slow his horse to increase the likelihood of a hit. Now the horses neck obscured most of Jack's vision, offering him no better target than the horse itself.

Jack was a moment from shooting the horse, with a view to levelling the odds, when the rider pulled his horse around to take what should have been a clear shot. Jack was bobbed down on his good knee, both to steady his aim and to make a smaller target of himself, yet still he felt like rat in a barrel.

The shot was loud; a singular noise as both pistols were fired together, only six or eight feet apart. It was, in the end, the Welsh terrain that won it for Jack. At that critical moment, as both men fired, the rider's horse stumbled on a loose rock, just enough to spoil his shot. Jack's shot struck him full in the shoulder, but it was no flesh wound. The rider landed dead weight on the rocky ground, spitting blood as he struggled for his last breaths.

Still crouched, Jack looked back. He didn't trust Elmshall's word. He quite expected he would have a musket trained on him. As it was, it was Jack that wished he had brought a rifle, as Elmshall trotted away, neither hurrying, nor looking back. Jack wasn't of a mind to shoot men in the back, but for Elmshall he would have gladly made an exception; a cold blooded murderer that even the French hated. He looked around at the three men he had killed, but they had only been carrying pistols and clubs. He considered riding him down, but with no knowledge of the terrain, coupled with the stories he'd heard of Elmshall's expert pistol shooting, he considered the odds would be loaded against him.

After a minute or so, he turned his attention to the dying man, who was slowly drowning on his own blood. He grabbed him roughly by his jacket and rolled him onto his side, in the hope of making him last long enough to talk. "It's all over for you. You know that, don't you," he said bluntly, but desperately. "You may as well bloody talk." Jack was gripping his Jacket aggressively, struggling to resist shaking him; such was his frustration that Elmshall had once more evaded him. The man looked back at him. His eyes looked so big and filled with fear. He spluttered and spat a mouth full of blood. "Your man knew I would kill you, but he let it happen, just for sport."

Jack lumped him back on the ground, looking back anxiously across the rocky hillside. He took his Jacket off and rolled it to form a rough pillow. "You may as well tell me. Tell me some bloody thing." Blood began to run down the corners of his mouth. He exhaled one last time, a single almost silent word being carried on that breath. "Thorn."

Chapter 8

Jack had made a quick search of the pockets of the three men he had killed. What he was looking for, he didn't really know. A proverbial pointing finger was his hope. Some sort of explanation as to who was doing what and why, but he knew it was never that simple.

As he expected, there was nothing. Glyn Marsh was the one telling piece of information he had, which tied Winter and potentially the entire South Wales revenue to Elmshall, but the question wedged in his head was 'what's it all about and how far does the poison spread?'

He pulled his knife from Marsh's throat as if he was taking it from a knife rack, casually wiping the blood from its blade, on a clump of grass. He sat beside the corpse and began to unpick the stitching on the hem of his trousers, to produce a small map, revealing his meeting point with Baker and Dewson.

It was barely a three mile ride, but on a weak leg, it had taken Jack more than half an hour to catch his mare and almost as long to work out the tiny map.

As the over grown road meandered to the row of cottages, the daylight began to fade. The first thing that struck Jack as odd was the lack of a church. Every village seemed to have a church of some description, even if it didn't have a clergyman to tend to it. This tiny hamlet was the opposite. It had its own priest, yet no church. As he surveyed his surroundings further, he huffed to himself for the lack of high ground. The cottages were positioned near to the bottom of a valley; a gift for an attacking force.

The sight of a woman taking water to a horse, grazing the rough track at the front of the houses, confirmed to him that he had got the right place. The horse was Dewson's; the calmest of animals, as steady and reliable as its owner.

"Good evening, Miss," Jack exclaimed, to attract the lady's attention. She turned sharply; startled by his presence. Her rugged face suggested 'miss' was a poorly chosen title. "I'm looking for Father Baker," he added, studying her features in more detail. Her teeth were blackened and her face drawn and narrow; her dress hanging over poorly covered bones. It was only as he dismounted his horse that he realised she was indeed, only a young woman.

"Are you with Cravith?" she asked with a nervous falter in her voice.

"No, Estelle. This is Jack. The man we've been waiting for," Bart interrupted from the doorway of the first cottage. She looked at Jack with suspicion; as if she'd already made up her mind about him.

"Bart," he exclaimed with delight. "What are you doing this far from the sea... This man is half fish, Estelle," he said loudly in the hope of raising a smile from the perpetually frowning woman.

"I had hoped keeping my distance from the sea might keep me out of trouble," Bart replied in a more serious tone.

"But you've found our smugglers for us," Jack replied, walking over to shake his hand.

"And they've found me. Us!" As Bart spoke, a boy of about five ran from behind a bush, into one of the cottages, drawing Jack's eye to the row of vegetable gardens at the front of the cottages. In one of the windows, he could see a woman looking out at him, her expression being much the same as Estelle's.

"Local women?" Jack asked, as two more women appeared from the end of the cottages.

"They are now," Bart replied sharply, before turning and walking back down the path. "We have tea," he mumbled.

"Tea would be good," Jack agreed, whilst conspicuously studying the women. He expected to see men's clothing on the washing line or work boots in the doorway, but there was no sign of men at all, other than Bart.

"How's the leg. I see you still limp."

"Stronger all the time," Jack replied, whilst still surveying the room.

"We have rabbit... This man's come close to hanging for a rabbit in the past, Estelle," Bart joked in the interests of banter. Estelle smiled weakly and unconvincingly as she tended to the boiling pot.

Jack grinned with pride, the poorest of pasts never being a source of shame to him. "I hunt for bigger prey these days."

"Lord Cravith?"

"Him and others. I had a run in with Major Elmshall today. The prey don't come any bigger than that."

"The woman killer? I wish Peter was here to see that."

"What have you got on Cravith?" Jack asked, being keen to know where he fitted in to what was beginning to look like a massive operation.

"Nothing goes on around here without Cravith giving it the nod. As soon as I started asking around, him and a bunch of his yes men tried to run us out."

"Us! You and Estelle?"

"And the others. He's the devil's hand, I'm telling you."

Jack smirked slightly. "What are they to you?" he asked gesturing towards Estelle.

"God's children, my parishioners," Bart snapped. "The most needy."

"I noticed you still wear the collar," Jack said, hinting at the impropriety.

"It's what's in here that makes a priest," Bart said, thumping his chest. "Not what he wears around his neck."

"As with all things," Jack agreed, in the interests of calming Bart's temper. "There's Dewson, out there. I must talk to him about Elmshall... Save me some rabbit, Estelle."

Jack hurried out of the back door, his priority being to bring an early end to the uncomfortable situation he found himself in. "Horry," he exclaimed, pointing to the back of an out building, for the purposes of a private conversation. "What the hell's going on with Bart?"

"You wouldn't think he'd got it in him, would you?" Dewson grinned as he spoke.

"What. Do you mean? Not all of them?"

"Saving their souls apparently, Jack Sir." Dewson sniggered and looked around the end of the building as if he was afraid of Bart. "Six of them in total... You do know what they are, don't you?"

"Women Mr Dewson, have you spent too long at sea?" Jack joked.

"Look at them closer... They're bloody whores. He sold them God and a new life along with it. Dirty bugger."

"Knowing him, he probably means it," Jack said in a more serious tone. "Whatever he's up to, I'm sure it's not like that," Jack assured Dewson, though having no doubt there was at least a level of impropriety concerning Bart's involvement with the women. "What of Lord Cravith?"

"I've asked around. Just the Lord of the manor type, as best I can tell, but then most people round here either can't or won't speak English. Awkward blighters, the bloody lot of em."

"So why is our clerical friend so sure he's running the smugglers?"

"He reckons he saw barrel loads of French brandy being carted into his house."

Jack puffed. "If you were Lord shiny boots, would you keep a load of dodgy grog in your own home? If you were selling it on, would you not keep it somewhere deniable; an old barn or somewhere?"

"I suppose. But Father Baker saw it."

"Then we'll ask, but Elmshall is running this. It stinks of him."

"What, the bloody Major from the Yarmouth thing?" Dewson said in amazement.

"Had a run in with him earlier."

"I'm sure you know best, Jack Sir, but this operation has been going on years. He must be new to it. He was a serving army officer until not long ago."

"We'll pay Cravith a visit, but there's a lot more going on here than just smuggling. I'd bet you a barrel of that French brandy on it."

Chapter 9

With a belly full of rabbit stew and a sense of bewilderment as to what was going on in the cottages, Jack and Dewson rode for the Cravith house.

It wasn't the same over indulgent statement of wealth that they were used to seeing in England. It was large, but rugged. Built onto a craggy hillside and surrounded by a rough dry stone wall, only large enough to keep livestock out, or in.

"It's a glorified croft," Jack grumbled, having expected something grander.

"What's the plan, Jack Sir?"

"We'll go and ask Lord shiny boots, over a glass of French brandy."

"Won't they do us in?" Dewson asked with concern.

"They'll try, but only if they're involved... Can't see it myself."

As they approached the rough wooden gate, two pigs grunted and ran back towards the house. "Are you sure this is it, Horry?" Jack asked, taken aback by the dilapidated state of the place.

"This is it, Jack Sir. Damned grander than them." Dewson pointed to a dozen stone and thatch hovels further down the valley.

"Damn it, Horry. These people aren't raking it in from smuggling. They're doing well if they get a decent meal in a day."

While Dewson got down from his horse to open the gate, Jack studied the group of houses along the valley. He could see people moving about; sheep being herded, even a late crop of hay being gathered in, and a man fixing the thatch on a roof. For a moment, his mind was taken back to a simpler time, when he could earn not always a days wage, but a decent meal for him and his granddad, for such tasks. They were times that now seemed magical to him, though hard and incredibly difficult at the time.

"There's somebody about," Dewson said, interrupting his daydream. "It's coming from round the back." The unmistakable sound of a cross cut saw began its almost tuneful hum.

They both walked their horses around the side of the house, following the sound of the saw. "Never expected to find pig shit in a Lord's garden," Jack joked as he guided his horse around the pig's wallow pit.

As they passed the corner of the house, three poorly dressed people came into view. A young woman was carrying logs into the house, while an older man and woman were working the long, two handled saw.

"Good morning," Jack said loudly, by means of making his presence know. "We're looking for Lord Cravith."

"Who wants him?"

"Jack Spoons. His Majesty's revenue."

The man immediately let go of the saw handle and picked up an axe. "I made your employer a promise the last time you people visited. I don't suppose anyone told you what that promise was, did they?"

Dewson pulled his rifle from his shoulder and lowered it to a firing position.

"Lord Cravith?" Jack asked in disbelief, as he put his hand on the top of Dewsons rifle and pointed it to the ground.

"I promised that the next revenue man that came here would be sent back, tied across his saddle... The King's of England gave this family the scraps, and on my life, that's all they're having back." As he spoke Cravith stepped forwards, putting himself within the axes swing of Jack.

"Jack, Sir," Dewson said nervously, prompting Jack for permission to raise his rifle once more.

"We'll both be dead before you draw the hammer back, Horry," Jack whispered, gesturing with his head to two more young women, standing ten yards to their right, pointing out dated muskets.

"God blessed us with daughters," Cravith said proudly as he swung the axe sideways, at Jack. As Dewson raised his rifle, the third daughter clubbed him across the back of the head with a log, knocking him senseless on the ground.

The first swing of the axe was easily avoided as Jack jumped back, causing it to miss its target, leaving Cravith exposed, just for a second. Jack lunged forwards, pushing the axe handle into Cavith's Chest and knocking him off his feet in the process. Cravith was like no aristocrat he had ever seen. He was as strong, if not stronger than any working man. With ease Cravith rolled over, pushing the axe handle up, under Jack's throat, forcing Jack to apply every ounce of pressure he could to resisting. Cravith was heavy; half as heavy again as Jack's skinny frame. The weight seemed to paralyse him, making his resistance useless.

"William," the older woman said softly, yet scornfully. In response, Cravith eased the pressure, just enough to allow Jack a clear breath.

"Why didn't you draw the pistol, boy?" he demanded. "They were your best chance."

Jack drew a breath. "I came here to talk. Not to fight."

"About what."

"The revenue, and the Priest."

"The bloody Priest!" Cravith growled, once more increasing the pressure on Jack's throat.

"William," Cravith's wife repeated, in doing so, controlling his anger.

Cravith at last drew himself back, jumping to his feet in a manner not in keeping with his size or age. "You can talk. Doesn't mean you're leaving alive."

Jack brushed himself off and slowly scrambled to his feet, orientating himself to his surroundings as he did so. "I'll have the pistols now," Cravith growled. "Don't know why a man would carry so much fire power if he doesn't intend to use it." Cravith pulled the pistols from their holster before Jack was fully upright. "Our Meryl clomped your mate a bit heavy... You better drag him in."

Jack and the girl who hit him, lifted Dewson to his feet, but he showed no sign of consciousness. "You have an army," Jack commented as he looked across the hillside to see men, women and children hurrying across, armed with farm tools and even a couple of longbows.

"I have many hungry mouths to feed, none hungrier than King bloody George."

"You speak treacherous talk, Sir," Jack said harshly, suspecting that Bart's suspicions may yet be proved right.

"I have an ancestral right!.. You see, many generations ago, some bloated King or other decided he wanted more land and my grovelling arse of an ancestor doffed his cap and marched off to France and set about it."

"Not much changes," Jack agreed, sitting Dewson in a roughly fashioned wooden chair in the middle of the kitchen.

"But that was it, you see. This poor stupid bastard did his bit for King and country. Town by town he took ground, while his King sat in England, getting fat. Then, just as it seemed they couldn't be stopped, they were. The French got their heads together. Two armies met and sprung their trap."

"What happened?" Jack asked, unexpectedly enthralled by the story.

"As his men fell to a sea of arrows and his flank was crushed by the largest cavalry he had ever seen, umpteen greats granddad called the retreat."

"I can't tell you how many times we've had to hear this story," Meryl complained as she dabbed Dewson's blood splattered head with a damp cloth.

"It's who you are, Girl. How you come to be here," Cravith grumbled back, in a manner that so reminded Jack of his granddad, back in Norfolk.

"The King did him in, I suppose," Jack suggested, enjoying the lighter spirit of the conversation, while it lasted.

"No. The King was crueller than that. He granted him these festering lands! We've been here ever since."

"Take no notice of my father. He loves this land and he tends to the people as if they're family," Meryl stressed with pride.

"And that is why we live like peasants!" Cravith added sharply, as if angered by his own actions.

"Every other landowner evicts those who can't pay their way to reduce their tax burden. My husband feeds and shelters them, like his father before him." Mrs Cravith walked over to the window and drew back the curtains as she spoke. "The Welsh do know how to show their appreciation, though." Outside, their other two daughters were explaining the situation to an amassed crowd of about thirty people, all armed with whatever had come to hand, and ready to fight for their Lord.

"It's a pleasure to meet you, Lord Cravith," Jack said boldly, whilst extending his hand in the hope of a fresh start.

Cravith looked at him and looked specifically at his hand. "Your friend. He's a soldier, plain as the nose on your face; the way he stands, like he's got a pike staff stuck up his arse, but you, I don't trust you, you're bad bloody news."

"I am, Sir, but I'm not your bad news... I'm investigating the South Wales revenue."

"Do you hear that, girls. Our guest has just started telling the truth... So what brings you here? This is the last place you'll find them sons of whores."

Jack didn't speak. He just pointed at two French brandy barrels.

"The Priest?" Cravith said in astonishment. "He would have seen the barrels, but he knows we're not bloody smugglers," Cravith lifted the lid in one of the barrels to expose its contents; salt. "Without salt we wouldn't all make it through the winter... If you're looking for answers, ask the Priest."

"He is one of us. Eyes and ears if you like. Why did you try and run him out?"

"One of yours? Then he's not a Priest?"

"In a manner of speaking," Jack replied, in an evasive tongue that could so easily have been the words of the Major, himself. "What's your problem with him?"

"We heard there was a Priest moved in, down in the vale cottages. A priest without a church, while we have our little church, but no Priest. It made sense to arrange something," Cravith explained, looking anxiously towards his daughter, considering what he could say or how he could say it. "I visited. Attempted to visit. Father Baker was fraternising with two of those women. Two of them!"

Jack smirked. "We had wondered," he said, failing to hold back a smile.

"You had wondered! Blast you man. For a priest to be allowed to behave like that, well it just can't be."

Jack dropped the smile from his face, realising the offence it was causing. "Father Baker was placed amongst the enemy more than once. Left to fight for himself and others before he was old enough to even have a choice and to add insult to a truly religious man, he was made a priest to gain access to a Spanish prison. I can not see fault in the man, no matter how many whores he associates himself with."

"If he wants to live like that, a life of a sinner, he must surrender his holy vows, turn his back on holy orders and beg for forgiveness."

"He may well do, but at the moment I'm more worried about the French and Spanish spies, I believe our mutual friends are bringing into the country," Jack said, being keen to shift the conversation to something more useful.

"Not my problem. Our people are hungry under an English King. We might do better with a French Emperor."

"Then I hope we don't meet on the battlefield," Jack replied, looking him in the eye as if he didn't fully believe him.

"I think he's coming round," Meryl interrupted, more to distract them from their increasingly heated conversation, than for any practical reason.

"You can't move him like that... Leave him here. He won't be harmed. You have my word on that," Cravith said coldly and to the point. "Best you get back to your whoring Priest."

Chapter 10

The presence of three horses, tied to the willow weave fence of one of the cottages was to Jack a worrying sight. It was only as he approached the first cottage and saw one of the women digging in the garden, that he felt able to relax once more. "Who's horses," he asked the woman, whilst studying her every feature and movement to try and understand how her former profession seemed so obvious to everyone else.

"More of your lot, from London, and a woman," she replied in her strong cockney accent, which seemed so out of place, both in Wales and in a garden.

Jack held his horse steady for a moment, still studying her. "You ladies and Bart... I mean, does he treat you all well?" he asked, failing to ask the question he wanted to, inhibited by extreme embarrassment.

"He treats us very kindly, Mr... And yes, we treat him kindly, too. That is what you wanted to know, isn't it?"

"If everyone's happy, it's none of my concern, Madam."

"None of your concern? I see the way you look. Like everyone else, as if we're something nasty, you've stepped in... Well Bart Baker's shown us a new life, free from hypocrites like you. He's given us pride; shown some of us God, even. Why shouldn't we show him our gratitude." She hissed with hatred as she spoke, her blackened and broken teeth on full display.

"As I say, Madam, It's none of my concern." Jack moved his horse off, refocusing his attention on the three horses. The bay, tethered nearest him identified it's owner, beyond doubt. It was the horse of Charlie Halfbasket.

"Charlie. I knew you'd turn up here, sooner or later," Jack boomed in welcome, as he stepped through the cottage doorway.

"It's Captain Halfbasket to you. Back stabbing weasel." Charlie had genuine hate in his voice, yet Jack smiled, considering it to be a big joke. "We have a matter of honour to correct, you and I, but it'll have to wait until this crap is out of the way."

"I'm not with you," Jack replied, taken aback by Charlie's venom.

"All you need to know is that there is a small army looking for you and Dewson. My friends according to what you've told Thomas Verance. More than once apparently." Charlie moved over to the window, looking out anxiously. Jack looked to see Bart calling in the woman he had just been talking to.

"You're a Lahand. You aren't telling me you don't know what the Lahands are," Jack snapped back.

"Where is Dewson?" Charlie asked, avoiding eye contact.

"He got hit on the head. I believe he's in good hands."

Charlie huffed, resisting a reply at first, instead kicking at a rag on the floor. "Bloody hell. I mean, it's not the fact that you suspect me... You called me friend, that's the thing, the thing that makes you a sneaky little bastard."

"And you, sneaking off to bed some Lord or other's geriatric wife. That's not sneaky. Especially with you having a wife of your own, and a child, is that right and honourable?"

"I don't answer to you, little shite, but when this is over, I'll see you out there, on that road and we'll settle it as if we were both gentlemen. That might be a struggle for you, I know."

"Best bloody way. One less Lahand in the world!" Jack couldn't believe the words he had just spoken. His hatred for the Lahands had finally and decisively prevailed over his friendship with Charlie.

"In the meantime you should visit the next cottage, and stay out of my bloody way."

Jack gladly turned his back and walked out of the back door and back in through the door to the next cottage which were no more than a foot apart.

"Bloody hell," he said with a gasp of surprise. "What does he mean bringing you here."

"The Spareson house wasn't safe, Jack," Camilla said as they embraced. "They're going for people's families. Their loved ones."

"That is you," Jack said, gripping her ever tighter.

"And you've got me in the bargain," a familiar voice interrupted from the darkened corner of the room.

Jack immediately released his grip on Camilla and reached for a struggling candle on the table beside him. As the candle's weak light illuminated the man's face,

Jack's suspicions were realised. "Afternoon, kitchen boy," Weaverton said, dryly.

"Snouty! I was assured your neck would be stretched by now."

"According to all the necessary paperwork, it has been," he said, swigging back on a hip flask. He looked so different to the last time they had met. Apart from being slightly drunk, he was rough looking. His hair was wild and dirty, and his clothes, tattered and filthy, as if he had been in them for countless days. "In the eyes of everyone that counts, I'm a dead man, and it seems, I brought disgrace upon my family in the getting that way!"

"Well you smell like you've been dead for a while," Jack joked as he shook his hand.

"I'd ask how you've been, but every picture tells a story," Weaverton replied, referring to his leg and his thickened and bloodied lip, from his run in with Cravith.

Camilla began to look and prod at his lip in the candlelight, while Weaverton got up from his chair to look through the thick curtains, which had been deliberately closed.

"A few smugglers won't be a problem," Jack assured him smugly. "It's closer to hand, what worries me."

"They weren't smugglers that we saw. They were soldiers in all but uniform."

"French?"

"Or Spanish. We didn't get close enough to find out." Weaverton walked over to the mantle-piece and began fiddling with a jar of flowers. "It's a wonder the things live at all, how little light they get, even when the curtains are open." Jack didn't respond. He just looked at him, knowing the man well enough to know there was something else on his mind. "Walls are paper thin you know!"

"I take it you heard my scrape with our Captain."

"I got most of it." Weaverton turned. His face more purposeful. "You do know the story of Charlie boy, don't you? Not that anyone other than yourself would be stupid enough to repeat it."

"I've heard no story," Jack said with deep concern.

"Well he wasn't likely to tell you, was he. Not exactly his proudest deed! The provost nearly court marshalled him over it, so you could argue, technically, you're right."

"What are you talking about," Jack snapped harshly, frustrated by the lack of actual information Weaverton was sharing.

"As you of course know, the Lahands are traitors, as are some of those they associate themselves with. From amongst these associates, a teenage Charlie Halfbasket was found a wife, and before he was twenty, a daughter was born." Both Jack and Camilla stood, enthralled by the story, which began to explain Jack's concerns, that he had held since the moment he discovered the family link. "So what happened, to bring the provost into it?"

"Charlie found letters. She had been acting as a go between... He passed the letters to my predecessor, but before she could answer to her crimes, he put her and the child on a ship to America, with every shilling he had." Having heard every word of their dispute, Weaverton took joy in sharing his knowledge of Charlie. It wasn't that they were enemies, though it was Jack who had broken his crooked nose. They were rivals, and Weaverton certainly wasn't going to miss a chance to get one over on him, when such an opportunity presented itself.

"Where do you want them, Mr," Estelle called from the road, where she stood with the boy, untying the horses from the fence.

"Put them in the first cottage," Charlie called back, as quietly as he could, to still make them hear.

"That's my place, that is. You're not putting horses in there," the woman in the garden shouted back.

"I doubt they'll make it smell any worse," Estelle snapped, to which the other woman went red in the face and stomped to the garden gate to meet her.

"We're all up shit creek if we don't get out of here," Jack growled furiously, hurrying from the room to confront Charlie. He barged through the door, back into the cottage, where he had left Charlie, hoping he had calmed from his rage. Charlie was now standing at the window with his rifle, doing his best to ignore Jack's presence in the room, watching Bart attempt to dissuade the two women from fighting.

"We've got to get out of here, Captain. We can't defend this place."

"We're already surrounded, Lieutenant. They'll hunt us like dogs if we run. Our only hope is to hide and let them pass." Charlie spoke deliberately coldly, not looking at Jack when he spoke.

"We've got to work together on this, else we're done for," Jack insisted. "I apologise if I spoke out of turn before, but we're sitting ducks, here."

"It's the best we've got," he said vaguely, refocusing his attention on a patch of bushes, some three hundred yards away. "You'd better get your rifle. The bastards are here." Charlie watched in horror as the two women began to fight on the road at the front; scratching, kicking and biting, as if possessed.

"If we show our faces now, we're done for," Jack whispered, looking over Charlie's shoulder at the two men, watching the fight from high up the hillside.

"Just keep quiet and out of sight."

"You don't really think they're going to miss that spectacle, do you?" Jack argued, as the two women brutally wrestled in the dirt. "You brought my woman here. Now I'm holding you personally responsible if any harm comes to her." Jack glared at Charlie as he spoke. "Dewson has walked that hillside, out the back. These are old mining cottages. Those hills are riddled with old mines; once we get amongst them, the boot's on the other foot... We're dead if we stay here."

Charlie rolled his eyes towards Jack, but as a matter of pride, did not speak.

"Bloody hell Charlie, you're going to get us all killed out of spite."

Charlie looked out of the window to see the two men slowly making their way down the hillside, their focus firmly fixed on the occasional flashes of flesh produced by the catfight.

"You can round up the whores," Charlie instructed him, grudgingly, at last moving towards the door.

The trees and bushes were still in full leaf, allowing them to disappear from sight in seconds, but that was only the beginning. Charlie knew there were quantities of the unidentified militia on the other side of the hill.

"I'm going to watch over Bart," Jack whispered to Camilla, as he sent her into the densely overgrown hillside.

"Jack," She said in a cautionary tone, to which he smiled broadly and turned back towards the row of cottages.

As Jack neared the back of the houses, he met Estelle; angry and looking the worse for a beating. She was heading for her cottage, closely followed by the boy, who Jack assumed to be hers. He afforded her little more than a passing glance as he continued to the back door of one of the middle cottages. He hobbled to one of the front windows; his weak leg suffering under the pressure and the speed of events.

It was as he feared. The two men, who took the appearance of road agents were confronting Bart on the road. A tall, scruffy man in a cloth cap grabbed him by the jacket and pushed him to the ground, while the other man pointed a musket at the woman, who was cowering on the ground, pleading for her life.

"There's no need to hurt the Priest," Jack called, as he walked down the path of one of the middle cottages with his hands held high. "His only part in this was to help a needy traveller."

"Shoot the bastard," the scruffy man instructed his companion, making a shooting motion with his hands, suggesting to Jack that the other man didn't speak English.

"No, wait. I can pay," Jack blurted frantically, knowing a shot would bring every one of Elmshall's men. The scruffy man put his hand up to halt the other man's shot. He smiled at the possibility of a bonus, on top of the price Elmshall had promised for Jack. The smile exposed a full set of perfectly straight teeth; mainly white, but for two, which were perfectly crafted gold. This was a man who, in his time, had seen wealth.

In that couple of seconds, and aided by the sight of the gold teeth, Jack put together a story, one which he was still making up as the words left his mouth. "I have gold... From the mines."

"That's bloody handy, when you're about to die, isn't it," the scruffy man seemed to be thinking as he spoke. "Don't worry, your corpse will be well robbed." He turned to his companion, once more to order the shooting.

"I only have a sample on me... My life for the mine."

"With two very slow fingers, lay the pistols down." He drew a sword and held it to Bart's throat, ready to react to any sudden movement that Jack might make.

"Walk slowly towards me," he instructed with tension in his voice. Jack had to assume he knew what he was capable of, from the corpses he had left the previous day. "What would you want with gold. You're a bootlicker, nothing more."

"Is that what Elmshall told you?" Jack said, slowly pacing towards him. "But then he's not going to want you to know about the gold."

"You're full of shit. There's nothing but coal in these stinking hills."

"Oh there is. This is pure gold." Jack slowly reached into his Jacket and flicked his knife with the sharpest twist of his wrist, hitting the musket man dead centre of the chest. He paid no heed to the scruffy man, trusting Bart to him. He dropped low and dashed to the musket, which the dying man was still trying to fire. As the man blindly jerked at the trigger, Jack pushed the musket to one side and wedged the thin skin between his finger and thumb between the hammer and the pan, before plunging the knife in further, right to the handle.

Only then, as the overriding adrenaline subsided slightly, did the pain from the musket hammer kick in. Much of the blood on him was from the musket man, but what was dripping from his hand was his own.

He eventually looked around to see Bart repeatedly bashing the scruffy man's head with a stone, despite the fact that he was long since dead.

"Hail Mary, Father," Jack exclaimed, in an attempt to calm him. Bart carried on. "BART," Jack shouted. "He's bloody dead."

The woman began to vomit at the sight of the flaps of skin, brains and shattered bone, which was all that was left of the man's head. Only then did Bart finally drop the rock, but there was no shock or horror at what he had done. He was hardened to it. That was him, that was what he had been fashioned into, as much as he wanted to be something else.

"Do you need to say some words over them?" Jack asked as he wrapped a cloth around his bleeding hand.

"No words," Bart uttered, turning his back on the mutilated body. "Just get them hid."

Chapter 11

The hour that followed the killings was tense. Six men rode through the village, stopping to look through the windows and steal food from the gardens, but the fact that the horses had strayed some half a mile, drew the militia away a lot quicker than expected.

Jack had taken Bart to hide on the opposite side of the valley, creating an area of crossfire, should they be discovered. "You knew Cravith wasn't involved when you sent that letter, didn't you?" Jack asked, as the two hid in the root pit of a fallen tree.

"The man was relentless, Jack. He rode up here again and again, quoting the bible and threatening all sorts of things." Bart seemed defiant, not his usual skulking submissive self.

"If you were any other man they'd have whispered about you behind your back and promised you a good dose of damnation and that would have been it, but you're a bloody Priest. It's a wonder they haven't strung you up by now."

"If those women are condemned souls, so am I. The church I follow speaks of forgiveness. What's the point in it all, if not. I've given it a lot of thought since Spain. I reckon a man like me, with some proper sins to forgive is closer to God than Cravith will ever be." Jack laughed instinctively, but Bart wasn't joking.

"By helping those women I'm surely redeeming myself, aren't I?"

"If you say so," Jack laughed. As much as he wanted to reprimand Bart for the trouble he had caused with Cravith, he remembered the state of despair he had previously be in; convinced of his own damnation. It seemed to Jack that Bart had found a way of reconciling his past deeds with his religious beliefs and made allowances for half a dozen whores in the process.

Jack was beginning to get restless. If it weren't for Camilla, he would have undoubtedly held his position until full darkness was upon them; the sensible, strategic thing to do. As it was, he was worried. If the militia did stumble across them, the situation would have been out of his hands and with Elmshall involved, that was a risk he wasn't prepared to take.

"Come on. We need to get you back to your ladies," Jack instructed Bart, prodding him with his boot, to move from behind the rocks. "We're no good to anybody here."

They slowly moved back down the hillside, towards the road that passed the cottages, being careful to stay behind rocks or bushes, where possible, in case the militia returned.

"Do you think you'll get a pop at Elmshall?" Bart asked as they reached the edge of the track.

"Not a chance; not here. He leads from the rear. We need to catch him when he's not expecting us, that's the only way to catch a coward like Elmshall." Jack bobbed down, behind a large bramble covered rock, on the edge of the road, just to study his surroundings. He waited a good two minuted, just watching for anything that could be the enemy, before eventually pulling on Bart's Jacket to be sure he moved with him.

It was only about fifteen feet of open ground, to cross the road, but in that time they were so exposed, should there be a straggler left behind from the main party of Elmshall's men. "Come on. We can't stay here," Jack insisted, once more pulling on Bart's Jacket. "We need to find the others."

Bart grabbed his hand and pulled him down, back behind a low gorse bush. "Look," he whispered sharply, pointing to just a single moving tree branch on the hillside, behind the cottages.

"It could be anything," Jack said dismissively, though maintaining cover.

"It could be, but it's not. It's a man, I'm telling you," Bart growled angrily. "You don't bloody think when that girl's around."

"At least I only have one to worry about," Jack muttered under his breath like a back chatting child.

The two remained motionless, just studying the area of the movement. A minute or so later a fleeting glimpse of a straw hat, confirmed Bart's argument, two men eventually appearing on the road at the bottom of the hill, on the far side of the cottages.

"Oh shit," Bart exclaimed as the two began to search the thatched outbuilding at the far end of the cottages.

"Language, Father," Jack whispered, just for the fun of it.

"That'll bring them back, sure as the heavens." Bart was watching as the men dug in the straw to find his cannon.

"We better find the others, before we get trapped here." Jack began to move, but cautiously, almost crawling to avoid breaking cover. He knew roughly where they'd be, but getting there unseen was becoming increasingly difficult.

"Do we need to kill them?" Bart asked, not timidly as would have once been his way, but in a matter of fact manner, as if it was no longer a big thing to him.

"We got lucky, before," Jack replied, giving him a long disgruntled look. "What the bloody hell do you want with a thing like that, anyway. Reluctant congregation was it?"

"There's cover and a better path over here," Bart replied, ignoring his comments. He'd found a tiny gorge, carved by a rock fall which ran up the hillside, giving them sufficient cover to reach the abandoned mines, unseen.

The route was quite steep and rocks continued to tumble beneath them, but the perilous path offered them sufficient cover to reach the mouth of one of the old mines, with little risk of being spotted. "Another bloody cave, Bart," Jack whispered with reference to the cave that had provided them sanctuary on the Gatekeeper's rock.

"Someone's beaten us to this one," Bart replied, pointing to a broken branch on the bush, which filled three quarters of the entrance.

Jack bobbed down, inspecting something that looked like a part of a foot print. "Come in and get out of sight, before you get us all killed," came the familiar, but angry voice of Charlie Halfbasket.

Jack and Bart scurried past the bush, into the darkest place imaginable. "They're still about," Jack said lightly, feeling his way along the mine wall. "Is it safe?" he asked, finding a crumbled pit prop as he went.

"It's a bloody sight safer than out there," Charlie snapped back. "They've already been past once."

Jack stared into the darkness trying to make out who else was in there and just how far back the old mine went. "We're all here, Kitchen boy, including Camilla," Weaverton said merrily, still being the worse for drink.

"What about Edith?" Bart asked with a voice full of concern. "She seemed distressed when she left us."

"That'll be from seeing what the hand of God can do," Jack grumbled, still shocked himself, by Bart's loss of control.

"You, of all people are in no fit state to judge me," Bart growled back.

"Judgement or not. We can expect the bloody lot of them back here on account of you keeping a cannon for a garden ornament," Jack replied angrily.

"It was hidden, and it was orders. I was told to hold weapons for emergencies. That's what I did."

"I'm sure Father Baker did for the best," Camilla said in her strong Spanish accent, which never failed to calm Jack's rages. "And Father, Jack's anger is born of his concern for his friends, including you, and you, Captain."

Jack looked again into the darkness, he could now almost make out her shape as his eyes acclimatised to the light. He found it incredible how a few words from her could so disarm, not just him, but Weaverton and Charlie as well, bringing necessary calm to the mine.

"Are we right to assume this Edith is still out there, somewhere?" Weaverton asked, once more swigging on his hip flask.

"Bloody hell," Charlie huffed. "What does she know."

"No more than that lot out there, I doubt," Jack said, after a long pause from Bart. "She doesn't know your purpose for being here, does she?"

"I don't know my purpose for being here," Bart snivelled in despair. "Never have done."

"We need to move off, Captain. Do you agree?" Jack exclaimed, purposefully putting Charlie on the spot, rather than risk him wasting time as he had done earlier.

"Well Father, you live here, what direction do we run?" Charlie asked.

Before Bart could speak, Jack spoke out. "We get help. I believe there is a man that might stand with us."

"Cravith?" Bart said in disbelief. "He's an animal."

"He's a Lord, with men more loyal to him than any King."

"He was ready to burn us out," Bart complained. "He's not going to fight along side us."

"Your enemy's enemy is your friend," Charlie argued half-heartedly, whilst deep in though. "Besides, he has Dewson. That's a rifle I want by my side."

Weaverton had consciously stood out of their debate, instead he moved through to the bush at the mouth of the mine. "Looks like Jack was right. There's a load of them just rode in." From the mine, they had a bird's eye view of the cottages and most of the road at the front. "They've got a woman with them," he added in a matter of face manner.

Bart pushed to the front, pulling a branch to one side with little care. "Jack, they have her," He said in a state of panic. "This is down to you, all of you, none of you would just let me be." He began to push and lunge, striking at Jack and Charlie, only missing due to his state of absolute blind panic, but every word he spoke was getting louder. Weaverton held a sizeable rock in his hand, debating in his own mind its worth with regards subduing Bart, without actually killing him.

"I know you're up there, somewhere. The woman's no good to me. Hand yourself over and she can go free." It was the voice of Elmshall.

"Shoot him, Charlie. You can make that shot," Jack demanded.

"And what then. None of us will get off this wretched hillside," Charlie growled, pushing Bart back from the mine entrance.

Weaverton took one last look at the jagged rock, which would undoubtedly have killed Bart, before swapping it for a loose pit prop. Bart lunged forwards, pushing between Jack and Charlie. With one, not particularly careful motion, Weaverton swung the prop, bashing it around the back of Bart's head.

"And relax," Weaverton exclaimed, patting the pit prop as if it were a cherished possession.

"You can bloody carry him," Jack said, refocusing his attention on Elmshall.

"Jack Bones," Elmshall called. "You of all people know what I'll do if you don't present yourself."

"How many do you make?" Jack asked Charlie, pressing his head hard against the mine wall in frustration.

"More than twenty. More than we can do anything about." Charlie turned, trying to see what was going on deeper in the mine. "Mind what you're doing back there, will you. You'll bring the rotten place down on us." He could hear rocks being moved, some tumbling, suggesting a small cave in.

"You won't want to know about the other way out, then," Estelle called. Charlie immediately began to walk towards the sound of the voices, only seeing the vaguest outlines of the women as he clumsily moved amongst them.

"Well Captain, I thought better of you," joked Helen, who was by far the largest of the women, Charlie having blundered into her, in the darkness.

Beg your pardon, Madam," he apologised awkwardly as he hurriedly passed her. As he continued, a vestige of light began to light his way.

"Ladies, you are a wonder," he exclaimed at the sight of a gap, little wider than a rabbit hole, which the women were prising rocks from.

"Captain," Jack called with a voice full of concern. "It's now or never." Elmshall had moved to the most prominent area of open space, with Edith. His sword drawn.

Charlie moved to the mine entrance, looking out. Elmshall had pushed Edith to the ground, holding her on her knees by the hair, his sword held high above his head in an almost ceremonial manner.

"May God forgive me. That shot would kill us all." As Charlie spoke, Bart began to regain consciousness. "Bring him. We have a way out," he instructed Jack and Weaverton, deliberately hurrying away from the mine entrance to avoid the miserable spectacle unfolding below.

Bart was still orientating himself to what was going on when he heard the heartbreaking scream of Edith's murder, echoing across the valley. That sound; that most terrifying noise stopped every movement in the cave, just for a moment, putting a tear in the eyes of the women and the boy, before they continued moving the stones with increased vigour.

For Bart that cruel killing represented something more. A turning point; a pivotal moment that would change everything.

Chapter 12

Their exit point took them out on the other side of the steep rocky hillside. It was a far more open landscape, dominated by sheep grazing.

Be it adrenaline or just the basic concept of self preservation, the women and the boy followed without a word, while Charlie led the party to a cluster of gorse bushes, a hundred yards or so down the hillside. At the rear, Jack and Weaverton carried Bart, sometimes almost dragging him. He was conscious; partially at least, but he seemed in shock. Edith's death was cataclysmic to him; another occasion in his life where he had done his best and it had ended in death.

"He's more of a woman than they are," Charlie complained, as they nestled amongst a cluster of rocks and gorse bushes, waiting for the last vestiges of daylight to vanish.

"He's the bravest man I know," Jack replied defiantly.

Charlie nodded in acknowledgement of the fact, which, with a little consideration, he already knew.

"Do you remember that day, on Drum's island... That's what they call it now, anyway... When you left there with your boots jammed full of gold," Bart spoke calmly, in total contrast to the raging rambling that had threatened to give away their position, only minutes before. "I took my share. I was sure that it would buy me a new life. I didn't know where, just so long as it was a worthy distance from those that had put me there in the first place." Bart's eyes were now fixed on the glow visible at the top of the hill, cast by the burning cottages. "A land agent contacted me. Understood I was in the market for a property, which seemed strange, but people talk, so I thought no more of it... He presented me with every property available to me. There were two! The first was them, a row of abandoned miners cottages in South Wales, or the second was a plot of land measuring six feet by two in an unknown location in Southern England."

"Tough choice," Jack replied with an inappropriate grin.

"You'll never be rid of them, Jack. Never."

"What would I do if I did?" Jack asked in all seriousness.

Bart never spoke, he just pointed to Camilla, who was in turn, listening to their conversation.

"He's right, Jack, you know," She began. "Your life's not long of this world if you carried on like you are."

He smiled and gripped her hand, amused as ever by her confused English, but not giving her words any deeper thought.

"As we've made it this far, I'd better give you your official orders, Lieutenant," Charlie said, interrupting Jack's conversation.

Jack looked at him for a moment, disappointed that the man he had once called friend was still only addressing him by rank. He broke the seal on the double folded parchment without speaking. It was the distinctive crown and daggers seal of the King's spy master, rather than anything that specifically identified Thomas Verance.

He squinted to read the words in the dim light. "I'm to provide you with any assistance you need to fulfil your mission," Charlie said, once more, coldly and with the tone of an officer addressing another officer.

Jack laughed to himself. "And I was just getting used to the Lieutenant thing. Reckon I'd have made a bloody good fat general, in about thirty years time." He refolded the letter and handed it to Bart. "My life, in your hands... I still trust you above anyone," he muttered, whilst staring Charlie in the eyes. "Does anyone know what the bloody hell the Thorn has to do with anything?" he demanded in a sudden burst of anger.

At first all were silent. Whatever was in that order was life changing, the truly shocked look on his face was testimony to that; nobody felt it appropriate to speak at first. After a good minute's silence, Bart eventually spoke.

"I've heard talk of the Thorn." He spoke quietly, looking down at his feet, as if afraid. "It's the ship that's bringing everything in. So some say."

"Jack," Camilla whispered softly, wrapping her arm around him.

"Lieutenant Bones and Weaverton, take a rear guard. All our troubles are behind us," Charlie ordered. "Ladies, try and keep low. We're going to try and get to the Cravith house without being seen."

"You can forget the Lieutenant, Captain. It's Just plain old Jack now. So you're going to have to think of something else to call me if you're so against first name terms." Jack spoke with venom and contempt. His orders seemed impossible, made more so by the fact that the man who was assigned to help would barely speak to him.

"You've been demoted," Charlie said in astonishment.

"I'm a bloody civilian, Charlie boy... You'll be getting no more yes Sir, no Sir, crap from me," Jack grinned with delight at the one faint silver lining to a very dark cloud.

Charlie paused. He took another look across the valley, just to be sure there were none of Elmshall's men on open ground. "Come on. They'll be widening there search, soon enough." Charlie moved out, hunched over to keep his silhouette to a minimum, the brightness of the evening not allowing dusk to fully give way to darkness.

As they moved across the only occasionally interrupted stretch of open ground, Jack and Weaverton hung back, each armed with a rifle, studying the hillside behind them for any sign of movement. Shouts and laughter from Elmshall's men, resonated from the burning shell of Bart's cottages.

"Their little party might just buy us enough time to get ahead of them," Jack said, optimistically.

"Or just maybe them bastards know they've got us," Weaverton said dryly. "Is it as bad as all that? The orders, I mean?"

"I'm still a bloody sight better off than you," Jack whispered, making a hanging gesture.

"I told you. I'm already dead, with the papers to prove it. King George can't hang me again." Weaverton smiled as he spoke, but there was a deeper sorrow in his face. Be it from the thought of the family he could never see again or the total destruction of his reputation; he was a troubled man.

Ahead of them, Bart, the women and the boy seemed to be huddled together as they moved; some of the women sobbing for their lost home. Only Camilla stood alone, constantly looking back to Jack.

"Jack," she whispered, allowing herself to fall behind the main party.

"I'll guard this side," Weaverton muttered, as he sidestepped to give them some privacy to talk.

She stroked Jack's arm, as if to display her concern. "What was the letter, Jack?"

"My orders... Once a criminal, always a criminal. Isn't that what you once told me, Snouty?" he called out to Weaverton.

"Absolutely. I'll swing on your bloody feet," Weaverton shouted back in the spirit of banter.

"What are you meaning?" she asked, with deeper concern.

"I might yet come out of the whole thing in profit, but I've lost my rank... I'm a wanted man again, Camilla," he said in a more earnest tone, to get across the seriousness of the situation.

"But why?"

"For the greater good, I'm told."

"Can't we just go somewhere?" Camilla asked with a whimper in her voice.

"We can, but not yet. There are those that wouldn't let us go."

"But why does it have to be you. Why can you not just bring a load of soldiers?"

"Panic, Miss. French soldiers on English soil; there'd be hysteria," Weaverton interrupted. "And next week they'd be coming in somewhere else. This is our one chance to catch them; to stop them."

"Besides, we don't know what the buggers are up to yet," Jack added as he ducked under the branches of the first of a cluster of trees, Charlie had led them to.

"But it's not we, is it Jack. It's them and you; Rib Bone Jack, the outlaw, when it suits them." Camilla's frustration was evolving into anger. A trait he had seldom seen in her.

"I would point out that I haven't come out of it too well, either," Said Weaverton. A comment they both ignored.

"Mr Vernance won't see me wrong, I know that," Jack argued defiantly. "I will find a way out and when I do, we'll want for nothing."

Camilla rubbed his arm in agreement, bringing an end to what was beginning to look like their first argument, before running ahead to hide her tears from him.

"That went well," Weaverton commented in his dry and sarcastic manner, as her crying became louder.

"Silence, please," Charlie ordered from the front, irritated by the constant whispering and whimpering of the women. "Keep down, out of sight, please." He felt unable to order them as he would a soldier, and as such, controlling the women was proving difficult.

"That's not right," Jack whispered, as he moved up beside Charlie, behind a cluster of rocks. "Something's happened." They were looking across the valley at Cravith's village. Torches were lit and people seemed to be moving around hurriedly, as if in panic.

"That's the curse of Jack Bones. Death wherever he goes!" Weaverton said cheerfully, as if it were a compliment.

"For a dead man, you've got a bloody lot to say for yourself," Charlie complained angrily.

"Well that's the thing you see Captain, that's all this dead man can do is talk," Weaverton replied with a drunken smile. "Nowhere to go. Nothing to do. No purpose!"

"I should have let them stretch your useless neck," Charlie snapped, increasingly angered by those he had found himself in charge of.

"I'm rather inclined to agree with you, but that's your Thomas Verance. Not the man the Major was... If he had no use for me, he'd have let me swing... I liked the Major!"

"Shall we pay his Lordship a visit?" Jack interrupted, before Charlie did Weaverton some harm.

"Elmshall will have left someone to watch," Charlie argued. "They'll be back in minutes."

"Then Cravith will have to choose a side. Looks like he's already had a run in with Elmshall, so his options are limited," Jack suggested, coldly and practically, which was a way becoming more routine for him.

"That's women and children down there," Charlie grumbled, knowing there was no other route open to him. "You'll have to do the talking as you've already met. He'll probably shoot me on the spot."

"May God forgive us," Bart muttered from behind, yet in a harsh manner, not befitting a clergyman.

Chapter 13

"Lord Cravith," Jack called, standing on open ground, a hundred yards outside the panic stricken village.

"You have a dozen muskets on you," a young Welsh woman's voice called back. "What do you want?"

"It's Jack Bones. We're here to help and to seek help in return."

"We don't want your help... It's you that brought this on us. We should shoot you where you stand."

"Last time I saw your villagers, they didn't have a dozen muskets, and if they did they wouldn't know which end to hold them by. We are here to help!" Jack studied the village behind her. Most of the torches had been put out, but he could still make out the outlines of people; mainly standing in full view as a show of strength, but the weapons they were holding were mainly longbows and farm tools.

"How many are you?" she asked as she began to pace forwards.

"I make it ten, including him," the unmistakable voice of William Cravith called from behind Jack.

"Sorry, Sirs," Dewson called. "We had to be sure it wasn't a trick. We've seen em off once already."

"Fall in Mr Dewson, unless you want to be put on a charge," Charlie ordered angrily. Dewson looked confused; his loyalties torn. He looked to Lord Cravith and most specifically to Meryl, who stood beside him. She nodded as if to give her permission.

"Lord Cravith. Elmshall and his men are bringing French spies and assassins into the country freely, and they are doing harm. With a few more people, this is our one chance to stop them." Charlie stepped forwards proudly and defiantly as he spoke, being sure not to show a vestige of fear.

"Why should we fight for you, for your King? Why shouldn't we give the other lot a chance?"

"They've attacked your village!"

"And they killed a man... We killed two of theirs. Seems more than fair... What doesn't seem right is the men that have left here to fight for your bloody King. For as long as any man can remember; sometimes by choice, sometimes by force, we've been losing people to the bloody Kings of England." As Cravith continued his rant, he lowered his musket, his rage increasing. Yet in contrast to his words, he seemed to be yielding. "This is Wales, Sir."

Charlie felt he should continue the argument as Cravith words were pure treason, yet he held a disapproving silence as Cravith turned and began to walk towards the village. "I suppose you'll be bringing the heretic and his Jezabels," Cravith grumbled as he walked back towards the village, not even glancing back.

"Lord Cravith," Bart called, stepping into open ground. "You are right. My actions and practices are not in keeping with the teachings of the church." As Bart spoke, he paced towards Cravith, infuriated by the label of heretic, inspiring Meryl to train her musket on him. "I have long believed that I am an unredeemable soul. Upon that we agree, but these women our different." Bart tugged and pulled at the white cloth he tied around his collar to denote his clerical status. "Yes they've fallen from the grace of God, but ours is a forgiving God and I believe that a man that can deliver them back to his flock may not be so totally lost, himself." Bart threw the collar on the floor, at Cravith's feet in the culmination of a rage which had begun to burn, since Jack's arrival at the cottages.

Cravith looked down at the piece of cloth by his feet. "Just a gesture, boy, but I believe this night may give you the chance to show your worth." Cravith looked past Bart as he spoke, to the hillside in the distance, behind his own house. A pair of burning torched could be seen progressing down the hillside, towards them.

"Don't you have anyone at your house," Jack asked Gwen, another of Cravith's daughters, once more puzzled by the unlordly actions of Cravith.

"The house has been sacked before, in my grandfathers day. It will rebuild... We could defend one or the other, not both."

"We could do with a few more aristos like him," Jack said, as he looked over her ancient outdated musket. "Will it even fire?"

"It has and it will again," she argued, with pride in the ancient matchlock musket.

"When it's empty, don't attempt to reload, unless you have time on your hands. Use it as a club. It'll probably be more effective like that."

"Mr Bones is right," Charlie announced to the group of men and women nearest them. "Good men are cut down by cavalry, whilst reloading good muskets. What you are reloading are little more than clubs anyway, so be ready... Form teams of two for bringing down riders. Work as a team and you'll both walk away, if one of you runs, you'll probably both die." Charlie looked with frustration, at the group of grubby faces staring back at him. "Do you understand me?" he demanded.

"Few of them speak English," Cravith said gruffly and with the disapproving tone that reflected his wide ranging concerns for the situation. "My daughters will translate."

"How did they fight, the first time they came?" Jack asked Dewson quietly, allowing him the freedom to speak. "It was just a skirmish, Jack Sir. Nothing hand to hand. Too early to tell."

"Who knocked over their two?"

"I did, Jack Sir."

Jack looked at the ground for a second, considering a different way to pose his question. "So how did they go on when Elmshall's men attacked?"

"Like fish in a net, Jack Sir. All flap and no think, but not one of them ran." Dewson spoke of them with pride. It was clear to Jack that regardless of the tensions between everyone else present, there was a strong bond between Dewson and those people; stronger perhaps even than his friendship with Jack.

"That's something," Jack agreed, distracted by the increased activity a couple of hundred yards past the

Cravith house. Their were now at least a dozen torches, in a cluster, suggesting a pre-battle meeting was under way.

"What do you think, Mr Dewson, shall we put their heads down," Charlie called across in an up beat manner, more in keeping with the Charlie Halfbasket Jack knew, before they fell out.

"Yes, Captain. I think it'll do em good."

The two took their rifles and walked as briskly as the darkness and the countless loose rocks would allow. The entire village watched as they vanished into the darkness, creating a tense silence as every soul present, waited for the shots and the subsequent reaction from Elmshall's men.

When it came, it was a single bang; both shots having been fired together, and two flashes some eight feet apart. Two more wild shots were fired back as Charlie and Dewson ran back to the cover of the village, but there was never any real likely-hood of a shot hitting home.

The torches seemed to scatter in panic, which was the point of the exercise, but more than that, the enemy morale was shaken, the mood of the villagers was raised as they watched the tiny, distant silhouettes of two men, drop.

Sure an attack was close, Jack looked for Camilla, who had been tending to one of the injured villagers. As he walked, he picked up a sturdy length of timber, which formed a workable club.

"You might need this," he said to Estelle, who was waiting at the door of the hut, where Camilla and Bart's women were gathered along with the wounded from the first skirmish.

"Is he with you?" she asked, looking anxiously towards the front of the camp.

"He has my rifle, he's an expert shot with it, and to defend you ladies, I have no doubt that he'll fight like a lion." She smiled back, but her thin face was racked with worry. Whatever it was with the others, there was something more between Bart and Estelle.

"Jack," Camilla exclaimed with joy as he appeared in the doorway. The two immediately embraced.

"Do you still have it?" he asked. "The pistol, do you have it?"

"Yes," she replied anxiously. "Do they come?"

"Soon," Jack replied. "I have to go, but know my heart and soul will be here, with you." He held her tightly, kissing her so fully as to attract the attention of each of the other women.

"My turn now," Helen joked. "I'm twice the woman she is," she boomed, pushing up her massive breasts to prove her point.

"Why is our flank so weak?" Jack demanded upon his return to the mocked up front line, no longer caring if he annoyed Charlie.

"You'll see my boy, You'll see," Cravith whispered, the pride in his voice giving away the fact that he had something planned for attackers approaching through the thinly spaced trees, to the left.

As Jack looked around him, his surroundings only lit by the natural light of the dim night sky, he saw shepherds and manual labourers, but more than that he saw determination. Though hidden behind carts and stacks of hay and clutching rough, out dated weaponry, Jack could see why the crooked South Wales revenue had left Cravith alone for so long. These were a people that would never run, because they had nothing to run to.

"That was expected," Cravith said flatly, not allowing an ounce of emotion into his voice, as he watched the mob throwing burning torches through the windows of his house. "We'll see your Major Elmshall dead before the night is out."

"Beg your pardon, Lord Sir, but Elmshall won't be coming within range. He's a coward, Sir. He'll be behind a rock somewhere, and if it doesn't go his way, he'll be back on that ship, Sir."

"William. Not will or Billy and certainly not Sir, not to my friends," Cravith said scornfully, irritated by Dewson's insistence upon rank and formality.

"Sorry Sir, I'll try to remember that," Dewson replied awkwardly, though clearly uncomfortable with the notion.

"How many do you make?" Jack asked with a grin, having had a similar conversation with Dewson when they first met.

"Twenty or so. By my reckoning that means about ten unaccounted for." As he spoke, Cravith gestured towards the wooded area to the left.

"Should we be moving people?" Jack asked with the appropriate concern.

"Keep one eye on the wood, that should be enough."

Elmshall's men began to mount their horses. They were moving slowly, confident in the knowledge they had all night, and that while they waited they were increasing the pressure on Cravith's civilian defence. They slowly trotted forwards in a single line, silhouetted against a drab night sky.

A single pistol shot was fired from the rear of Elmshall's line. An obvious signal, yet the riders continued to move forwards unnaturally slowly. The only light from them was now the glow from a pipe, as one of the men had one last smoke before battle.

A loud yell from the woodland came suddenly, sending a shock wave through the defence of scared men and women, as even those seasoned to battle, jumped or gasped.

"Bear traps," Cravith said with a wry smile. "Some of them may reach us, but it won't be a coordinated attack."

As Cravith spoke, Elmshall's riders quickly moved to a gallop. Dewson and Charlie, being the best rifle shots stepped out from each side of the hay cart, each removing one from the saddle, but the dozen or so shots that followed didn't touch them.

It only seemed like a second before all that could be seen was the blackness of horse's chests charging from the darkness, bearing down on the small army of farmers. The layout of the hay carts funnelled the riders through two gaps, causing two bottle necks which seemed to draw the riders in.

Jack waited until the last second; until they were actually coming through the gaps, before he fired his pistols. He stood upright and took careful, unmissable aim, hitting the rider nearest him, but to his frustration, not removing him from his saddle. He swapped pistols, so as to still be using his favoured left hand, but as he took aim at a second rider, coming through the gap, his view of his target was interrupted. Cravith's people quite suddenly stormed forwards, armed quite specifically with pike staffs, wedging the handles in the ground, halting the horses in their tracks.

As horses reared up, two men fell from their horse, almost instantly being pounced upon and stabbed, not by the men, but by the women, who seemed to make up the bulk of this particularly effective counter-attack, including Cravith's wife and daughters.

Before firing his second shot, Jack scanned the battlefield, in the faint hope of seeing Elmshall amongst the shadows, but Dewson's take on the man was right; he was nowhere to be seen.

It was the injured, high pitch scream of a woman that identified Jack a target for his second shot. A man in a straw hat seemed to be leading the attack on one of the two gaps, and making progress. Jack rushed over, shooting him from the saddle as a matter of formality; his focus being on a woman, laying outstretched on the ground in front of him. It was Mrs Cravith.

"Ellen," Cravith called, running from the other side of the blockade. Jack knew this could change everything. If their vital ally lost the will to fight, they would have no option but to fetch soldiers and trigger unimaginable national panic.

Cravith looked down at his wife in despair as she laid fully conscious, with a massive cut running diagonally across her chest. In a sudden fit of anger, he picked up the pikestaff, which laid behind her and threw it with all of his great strength, and a good measure of anger, striking a horse in the neck, bringing both horse and rider down.

"Someone get the priest," one of his daughters called.

"NO," Cravith boomed. "Such a man would guide her straight to hell."

"But her rites, Father," the daughter sobbed, kneeling beside her mother, clutching her bloodied hand.

"We will all pray. God will hear us, as I'm sure he has for all the other souls we've lost, without a priest." Cravith spoke strongly as the leader that he undoubtedly was, but the despair in his voice couldn't be hidden.

With Elmshall's men retreating, Bart came over anyway. He pushed his way to the front of the gathering of villagers who looked on, genuinely grief-stricken by her impending death.

"Be gone with you," Cravith growled at him.

"Mr Baker has other skills, Sir," Charlie insisted, before beginning to quite roughly guide as many people as he could back to the blockade.

Cavith gripped Bart's shoulder firmly, still refusing to let him near his wife. Jack Knelt down beside him. "We came back from Spain on a hospital ship. Every injured man from a heavy fight was on board, with just one doctor. The ship's priest wouldn't allow Bart to practice, so he assisted the doctor. Two weeks in the doctor fell ill... The doctor was one of the very few men to die on that journey, but our man, here, he worked on injuries like that for eighteen hours a day."

Cravith looked Jack in the eyes, as well as he could in the poor light, just to gauge the honesty in his words. He tentatively released his grip on Bart's shoulder, but watched his every motion.

Bart picked her dress away from the wound, being careful not to either expose her breast or touch her any more than was necessary. Cravith looked on, only ever a breath away from dragging him away.

"Let him try, father. Please," Meryl begged.

Mrs Cravith was breathing heavily, but irregularly.

"Her lungs are cut, any fool can see that," Cravith snarled, standing up and turning his back for just a second to try and compose himself.

"I don't think they are. It's a bad wound but we should be fighting for this woman in this life, not the next," Bart argued as he held a small lamp over the wound.

"Get everyone of those muskets loaded," Charlie bellowed, frustrated by the people's sudden lack of interest in the enemy. "This woman is obviously important to you, so stand and fight for her," he demanded. His words were followed by a series of Welsh whispers; the few English speaking villagers, translating.

"Sit her up. We need to push this shoulder forwards," Bart instructed her daughters. "It will slow the bleeding."

"Jack," Camilla called from the huts. "Can you help?.. It's Horry." He looked out across the valley, uncomfortable with leaving the blockade.

"Is it bad?" he asked, looking back one more time to see Charlie assigning people to positions; bellowing his orders as if they were all enlisted men.

"He's shot, Jack."

Once more Estelle was at the door. She was armed with the pistol Jack had given Camilla; something that didn't trouble Jack. He could see it in her eyes that she wouldn't hesitate to use it, where as Camilla was still haunted by the officer she had killed on the Gatekeeper's rock.

"It's deep," Flow said with worry, dabbing at the wound in his side.

In contrast, Helen cackled, her eyes full of unspoken suggestion.

"Is nothing serious to you?" Estelle snapped from the doorway.

"Ladies, please," Jack said in his best officer voice. "How'd you catch that bugger, Horry?" he asked just for something to say. Dewson was laying on his side, biting on a leather belt against the pain and in no state to be making light conversation.

"Did you want to take his shirt off, Helen. I know you'd like that," Jack said, encouraging her in her lecherous banter.

"Oh, yes. Let's be having you, Mr Horry," she joked as she gently pulled it from his arm, to expose his back.

"Shit," she exclaimed, her joking manner at last subdued. "What happened to him."

"They're flogging scars. More than any man should carry."

"Why," Camilla said with horror.

"A good officer, like Charlie, commands respect, and everything else follows. A bad officer, like Elmshall, can command anything but respect. Officers like that, compensate with the whip," Jack explained, as he mopped the blood away to reveal the exit wound.

Camilla put a hand on Dewson's shoulder, in sympathy.

"The shot went straight through. If you ladies can stop the blood and keep it clean, he should be alright." Jack handed Camilla a rag as he spoke, but he couldn't take his eyes off the scars on Dewson's back. "Who did that. Was it Elmshall?" Jack asked, knowing Dewson and Elmshall's paths had crossed, before Elmshall had been exposed as a traitor.

"No. Not directly. He was one of many honourable men that could have stopped it, though," Dewson muttered through the pain.

"What did happen?" Jack knew he should just leave it, but he needed to know. The wounds explained so much about the eccentric, over obliging nature of the man.

"I'd only been enlisted a couple of weeks... Me and a few of the lads found a local alehouse near the camp. You know how it is." He stopped for a moment, wincing from a sudden burst of pain as Camilla pressed hard on the wound. "It was a pair of snotty young officers, three parts pissed, Jack Sir... Started pulling rank, showing off to the tarts... No offence, miss," he added, realising Helen was listening in. "Long and short of it is, they wanted some poor sod to stitch up, and I was the idiot too green and stupid to salute."

"They did that for not saluting a drunken officer?" Helen said with disgust.

"By morning I'd pulled a knife on em; their word against mine... They were ready to string me up, if it weren't for General Alderton. He didn't like them or believe them, but an officer's word is worth more than a regular soldier's and against two of them, I was a dead man."

"That's bloody wrong," Helen huffed. "How'd you dodge the noose?"

"Alderton was a deeply religious man. He put it in the hands of God. He ordered enough lashes to kill, but if I lived through it, I was an innocent man."

"In the King's army," Jack exclaimed. "I don't wonder the Frenchies are making idiots of us."

"Trial by fire, he called it... Story goes General Alderton made a small fortune out of the wagers on me surviving."

"I once heard it said that God was a gambling man, and we are dice. Makes a lot of sense when you think about it," Estelle interrupted from the doorway.

Chapter 14

An hour had past, and to everyone's astonishment Lady Cravith was still alive.

Elmshall's men had gathered at the burning shell of Cravith's house, waiting, expecting the poorly armed civilians to run. As it was, every man, woman and child stayed; each with their post and their own vital part to play in whatever was to follow.

"How did you come across bear traps, Sir?" Jack asked to serve his own, sometimes dangerous curiosity.

"My father. There was a blacksmith in Tenby. He'd been making them for the fur trade, in the frontiers. One day they just stopped buying. Left him with a cart load. My old dad was a crafty man, he knew the blind spot, that stretch of wood posed, even then, so he bought the lot."

"Clever man," Jack agreed, as he fiddled with a pair of sheep shears, pulling at the handle, deliberately trying to break them in half. "Bloody perfect," he said, with a sense of achievement as they broke into two equal sized single blades.

"Your preacher is a talented man. I owe him my wife's life."

"He's a good man, but he needs help seeing it."

"There's a place for good men here. Even Englishmen!" Cravith smiled slightly to share the joke, but there was purpose in his words.

"Where did they come from?" Jack pointed to the thick metal breast plates, worn by two of the women, standing at the cart.

"Civil war. Not sure if it ever ended around here."

"Won't stop a musket."

"No, but it gives them a chance against a sword or a pistol," Cravith explained, before returning to his wife's side.

It was now deep into the night, but with hours before dawn, there was no need for Elmshall to hurry. The waiting was doing more harm to morale than any number of musket shot could. Women and children were sobbing, and the men were jumpy; put on edge yet more by every sound and movement in the dark.

"Listen up people," Charlie bellowed, sensing the need to distract them from their fear. "We picked up some scratches and scrapes, but last time they came, we didn't loose anyone. They lost six. They're more afraid than we are right now. If every one of you stands your ground; holds your position, I promise you we will win this." A few of the villagers gave a half hearted cheer, but the idea of facing the same concentrated assault again filled them with dread, and it showed.

Jack looked back to Camilla as she attempted to make Lady Cravith comfortable. Once more he had put her in harm's way, though, as ever, unintentionally. He looked back to the large hut, where Dewson and the other wounded were being treated. The women were coming and going, hurriedly fetching water and fresh cloth and blankets from the other houses. Charlie's words thinly veiled the truth, that though they had gained no more deaths since the raid in the afternoon, so many of those peaceable people were quite badly injured, leaving the blockade poorly defended.

"Where's Baker boy?" Weaverton asked, in a more sober manner than Jack had seen of him, since he arrived in Wales.

Jack pointed to the house where the injured were being treated. "He'll do more good than us tonight."

"The boy's full of surprises," Weaverton muttered with a sense of irony.

Keen to distract his own mind from the next attack, Jack considered a question that he'd never, in their past encounters, thought to ask. "What's your first name? I've never heard you called by it."

"There's two reasons for that," Weaverton said without cracking a smile. "First reason is that nobody ever wants to know me well enough to call me by my first name."

"That I can understand," Jack happily agreed, in the constant spirit of banter that existed between them. "What's the other reason."

"It's bloody daft!"

"As you're still half pissed, I was hoping you'd tell me what it is," Jack persisted.

"I may as well. Since Romulus Weaverton is a dead man, I've got to find a new name anyway."

"Romulus?"

"A twin, you see. You'll never guess what my brother was called!"

Jack smiled politely, assuming it to be some kind of religious reference of which he had no idea about.

"What do you reckon, Captain. Do you think they'll try and come around the back?" Jack asked as Charlie joined them, behind one of the hay carts.

"No, they've had a taste of his Lordship's bear traps, besides, they know we're on our last." Charlie gestured towards the handful of people left on the blockade. "We've brought them misery, same as we do everywhere we go."

"We could take the fight to them?" Jack suggested.

"I'm thinking much the same," Charlie agreed solemnly. "If we holed up in that bunch of rocks out there, his Lordship's people could still give covering fire."

"Dewson is in no fit state and Bart's worth too much to these people," Jack said, working out the likely odds in his head.

"If it takes the fight away, my daughters will command the blockade. I'll fight with you," Cravith exclaimed, having been listening in on the conversation.

"And I make five." Bart called from the back of the camp. "It'll be a more holy fight than any I've fought before."

"You have penance to serve, Mr Baker. You are going nowhere," Cravith said sternly, knowing his wife's chances were so much better if Bart remained.

Jack was keen to avoid goodbyes. He walked to Camilla and hugged her firmly, without speaking a word. He was only going a hundred yards away, and to have made too big of an issue of it would to be accepting the poor odds they faced.

"Keep every musket firing," Cravith instructed Meryl, whom, despite being one of the younger daughters, seemed to be the one giving the orders, as her father prepared to leave the blockade.

Cravith bobbed down to his wife, clutching her hand. She smiled back. "Our ancestors would have been proud," she whispered.

"I'm proud," he said, before kissing her on the forehead.

The four hadn't been to their new position for any more than five minutes when the thundering of horses hooves began, once more. The night was darker now, shrouded in cloud, which had the effect of extinguishing the moon and stars almost completely.

"Wait until we have a clear shot, however close they need to come for that to happen... If we each drop one with the first volley, we might have a better chance." Charlie's instructions were, as they had to be, directed at equals, rather than subordinates, particularly with Lord Cravith amongst them.

They each watched anxiously into the darkness, waiting for that first sighting, to see how many they faced. "Remember, every shot needs to hit home," Charlie whispered as he trained his rifle on the valley ahead, sure of their appearance at any moment.

Jack laid his pistols on the rock in front of him, for speed, before cocking his rifle, but with the click of the hammer, the galloping stopped. "Where the bloody hell are they?" Jack asked with frustration.

"Don't wish them on us, kitchen boy," Weaverton muttered, now fully alert, having run out of brandy for some hours.

"I think I preferred you pissed," Jack grumbled back.

"There's an old pit out there, from my grandfather's day. They won't stay there for long. They'd be sitting ducks," Cravith explained.

"They're having another go, around the back," Weaverton suggested.

"No. He won't make that mistake twice, but why loose the momentum of the charge?" Charlie asked, more as a matter of thinking out loud, rather than for the input of others.

"They're not going to attack... The Frenchies have refused to fight," Jack said with certainty and confidence. "Cowards, led by a coward."

"Then what are they doing there?" Charlie asked with an air of contempt at the suggestion.

As if to answer his question, a strong Welsh voice began to shout out a message in Welsh. The words echoing across the valley were directed at the Welsh speaking peasants of the village.

"What's he saying?" Charlie instinctively asked.

"They're offering safe passage for anyone who wants to leave," Cravith explained, whilst looking at Jack in an unspoken acceptance of his suggestion.

"Will they leave?" Charlie asked earnestly.

"Not one of them. It's their home; proud Welshmen, every one of them."

"Then we wait it out and hope you're both right," Charlie replied, flattening the ground behind his own personal rock, in anticipation of a long night.

Chapter 15

By dawn the valley was deadly quiet. It seemed that even the birds sensed the tension as the dawn chorus was struck silent.

As the first weak light shone through the trees, onto the entrenched villagers, words were still only whispered, and even then they were few. It was only as the four men, from the cluster of rocks, began to walk back, boldly and on open ground, that anyone felt able to relax.

They walked in a line. A forgotten nobleman, a disgraced aristocrat, a distrusted senior officer and Jack; a young man who had spent most of his life on the wrong side of the law.

"Post lookouts on the high ground. They've gone, for now at least," Cravith instructed Meryl, who stood at her post, behind the hay cart, with Horry Dewson beside her.

As he neared the blockade, Cravith's pace quickened. He skipped over the shafts of the cart, such was his hurry to learn the fate of his wife. "Dad, she's fine. She's going to live," Meryl assured him.

"Stand down, Mr Dewson," Charlie ordered, shocked to see his boots soaked in blood, where it had ran down his leg, from the stomach wound.

"I've begged him to rest, but he's refused to go anywhere until your return."

"Well we're back you stupid bugger," Jack said, lifting him by one arm, while Weaverton took the other.

"Get Baker to look at him immediately," Charlie bellowed, upon the sight of the large patch of blood he had left on the side of the cart, where he had been slumped for some time.

"He will be alright, won't he?" Meryl said, with no less concern than she showed when her mother was injured in the night.

"It would do him good to have his own nurse," Charlie said, guiding her gently by the shoulder to follow them.

As he made his way to the hospital hut, Jack studied the faces of the villagers he passed on his way. There was a language barrier, but he had overcome that before, when he met Camilla. Their thought's were clearly written on their faces. Their accusing stares put the blame for their misery squarely at his feet. He could only guess what had been said, in their own tongue, but he knew the air of blame and contempt was directed at him alone.

The scene that awaited him as he entered the one room hut, explained to him just why their attitude was so hostile. It was impossible to cross the room without walking around several injured men and women, who had been made as comfortable as possible on blood spattered sacks of straw. He froze in the doorway, just to take in what he was seeing. More women than men laid injured, but that was to be expected as several of the men had already gone to war in the previous years.

One thing he had learnt; Welsh women fight quite as fiercely as any man. It didn't make seeing them lying in their own blood, nursing sword and shot wounds, any easier, but he felt an intense sense of pride and admiration for the people of that village, and no amount of resentment they could direct back at him would change that.

"Jack," Camilla called from the back of the room, where she was ripping cloth into bandages. "Have they really gone, Jack," she asked, her enthusiasm making her strong Spanish accent difficult to understand.

"We think so," he replied, stepping over the legs of Mrs Cravith, who laid, unconscious, with her husband watching over her, anticipating her every breath, silently praying it wouldn't be her last.

"Still none lost?" Jack asked Bart, as he hugged Camilla.

"None, Jack. Nor will there be, if I can help it." Bart was sewing up the shot wound on Dewson's side, assisted by Helen, who's dress was soaked from top to bottom in blood.

"I'm sorry I brought this on you," Jack said apologetically, to Cravith.

"I picked a side; the same side this family has been choosing for centuries, and for the record, I'm glad I did," Cravith said, considering his words carefully. "You were right. Whatever happened, the fight was always going to come to us." Cravith wasn't looking at Jack when he spoke. His gaze seemed fixed on Bart's needlework. "They say you learnt that on a war ship?" he eventually asked as Bart tied off the thread.

"On the journey home, Sir. Our transport was jammed solid with injured men."

"Any fool can pray," Cravith began, getting up to walk over to him. "We have bibles, we have long took care of that for ourselves. But a doctor; that we need, here and the other villages."

Bart looked at him blankly, as if he thought he was talking to someone else.

"Our nearest doctor is in Tenby, and he refuses to leave town... You have a gift. I believe God sent you to us for a reason."

Bart still didn't immediately speak. The idea seemed to him absurd. He looked at the floor, considering an answer that wouldn't offend Lord Cravith.

"If it's books you need, I can get you all of that... I am a bloody Lord, you know," Cravith added with frustration. "And have as many nurses as you need, if that's what worries you, so long as it's not in the name of our Lord."

"It's not that, Sir... When I was too young to have a choice in the matter, I was enlisted to something that will surely follow me to the grave. Nobody escapes that... I've tried," he exclaimed with a sense of deep sorrow.

"That's a terrible pity, young man, but you might not have any choice in the matter. God is more powerful than King George, you know." Cravith smiled slightly, as if to make a joke of the statement, but to Jack at least, it was clear he wasn't giving up on the idea, that easily.

Jack gestured to Camilla to step outside as she neared the door. "You know I have to finish this, don't you," He said as they embraced.

She nodded with the most sad and serious face. "Will it ever be finished, Jack?" she asked.

He hesitated, before wrapping his arms around her waist. "One day, soon. I swear it," he assured her. "But it won't be to the life of a peasant."

"Jack. How many rich men have you seen killed?" she pleaded.

"Not nearly as many as I have seen, poor men!"

"So, where is this great wealth to be coming from?" she asked with an uncharacteristic air of sarcasm.

Jack smiled. "Call it back pay. King George never did give me that first shilling!" Camilla didn't return his amusement. She considered his joking attitude and the lack of a straight answer, offensive. She wriggled free from his grip with some force, before charging back to the hospital hut in a flustered state.

"Nicely played, kitchen boy," came a voice from the darkness.

"What do you want?" Jack grunted at Weaverton as he emerged from behind the bush, where he had been lurking.

"Just a tiny piece of what you've got would be nice.

I'd settle for a name I dare speak, for starters."

"What's wrong with snouty. I always liked that, for you!" Jack replied in such a dry manner that it was impossible to tell if he was in any way serious.

"With the absence of a name, I was wondering if you ever worked out where our Lordly host kept his brandy." Weaverton waggled his empty hip flask as he spoke; his hand quivering slightly from the need for it.

"I'll find you a bloody name, and something to do with it," Jack replied sharply. "Next person through the door. Agreed?"

"Agreed!"

They waited, as various people neared the door, but failed to come out. "It'll surely be something I can't even say. They're all bloody Welsh," he said nervously. "And I refuse to call myself after him," he added sharply, as Bart approached the open door.

"Pardon me, Sirs," a young Welshman said timidly, as he carried a pale of water in from the well.

"Of course," Jack said with a wry smile, stepping back to allow him in. "Do you mind me asking your name?"

"I'm sorry, Sir, if I spoke out of turn," he began, in genuine fear.

"No. You've done no wrong. We were just saying, weren't we Snouty. That lad fought well last night. We'd like to commend your name to his Lordship."

"We did indeed," Weaverton agreed, tucking his empty hip flask back into his jacket.

"Edwin Jones, Sir. Thank you, Sir," The youngster said with glee.

"Well, what are the chances? My friend here is Romulus Jones. Maybe you're related," Jack added, just to annoy

Weaverton, who would have once treated such a man as if he were something unpleasant he had stepped in.

"Very pleased to meet you, cousin," Weaverton said, extending his hand to shake his, just to make a point to Jack.

"Who'd have thought it. The biggest snob I've ever met; akin to half the peasants in Wales!" Jack revelled in the idea, but it didn't seem to bother Weaverton. His attitude towards all people had changed beyond recognition, from the snooty aristocrat Jack had first met at the Spareson house. "Before this is through, I'll have a title for you, to go with the name."

"Too much kindness," Weaverton groaned sarcastically, before retrieving his empty hip flask once more, as a nervous reaction to what was to him an uncomfortable chain of events.

"Let's have a look over here, Romulus," Jack said smugly, gesturing to a selection of out dated weapons, which had been laid out for the people to choose from, the night before.

"Did anyone ever fight with that stuff?" Jack asked, fascinated by the heavy armour and maces which laid on the ground in front of him.

"That's the worst of it. The pikes and the fun stuff, people have still got. Why, were you thinking of a change of tools?"

"Weighs a ton," Jack said, picking up a civil war breast plate.

"They reckon half an army drowned wearing them, across the water. Just goes to show, your enemy isn't always what you think."

Jack looked at him enquiringly, considering his words carefully for a moment, before concluding that he was still slightly drunk. "I take it you'll join me back in Tenby?"

"Nowhere else to go, unless I stay here with my new cousins!"

"Might stop a shot, if you're lucky, but you're not moving very fast in that,"Charlie said as he walked over. "A couple of the villagers have heard talk of a bay, where it's all brought ashore, and some old buildings and the like where our French guests might be staying... Only two or three mile round the coast from Tenby." Charlie's words were put across as a statement rather than an order or a question. With neither man under his command, that is all they could be.

"Sorry Charlie. I've business in Tenby," Jack quickly replied.

"You are still in the service of the King?"

"I am, and I have my orders," Jack replied sternly. "And they have nothing to do with apprehending French soldiers on English soil?"

"Welsh rock, if we're being accurate," Weaverton interrupted, causing Charlie further irritation.

"Mr Verance is a gardener now. Did you know that?" Jack said with a glint of mischief in his eyes.

Charlie huffed in response, enraged once more, by what he saw as a personal betrayal.

"Point is, while you're pulling the leaves off the weeds, one by one, I'll be pulling it out by the roots!"

"And how do you intend to do that?"

"That, I can't tell you," Jack said hesitantly, knowing that his words would infuriate Charlie further.

"We stand and fight Frenchmen, shoulder to shoulder, yet you still refuse to trust me," Charlie snapped back.

"While Elaina Crass is out there, even the truest patriot can be turned," Jack replied in the same calm tone.

"Amen, to that," Weaverton once more interrupted. "And may the heavens shit on you, Fraser!"

"Where are the rest of the Sparesons?" Jack asked, just to calm Charlie's fraying temper.

"Elsewhere! And the recruits are in your alehouse, protecting the Verance family and yours... If I bring regular soldiers into this, the word will be out; the country will be in panic." Charlie kicked a small rock at the hay cart, just to vent his anger; an act that must have hurt his toe, if he would but admit it.

"Are they actually there?" Jack asked with concern. "Mrs Verance spends most of her time with her mother, in Suffolk, as I understand it. His daughter too."

"They will be well guarded, I assure you."

"Good to know, Captain," Jack agreed, before awkwardly bobbing down to look over the weapons in more detail; his injured leg suffering from the strain of the night before.

Chapter 16

Jack and Weaverton had set off, quite deliberately, an hour before dark, to a less warm farewell from Camilla than Jack had expected. Their destination; Tenby, was the last place Elmshall would expect them to emerge. With both Elmshall's men and Winter's revenue informally patrolling the streets, it was, on the face of it, a foolish, if bold move.

"So, what's our cover? Who are we, if anyone asks?" Weaverton asked as they rode past the first row of rough thatched cottages, which marked the outskirts of Tenby.

"I'll talk. You agree!" Jack smirked slightly, amused by the workings of his own plan.

"Just follow the kitchen boy," Weaverton muttered to himself, before reaching into his jacket for his flask.

"I thought that thing was empty," Jack complained.

"A generous benefactor," Weaverton exclaimed, raising the flask above his head as if to toast the supplier. "Turns out one of our village friends has a little boat... I was hoping for French brandy, but Irish whisky comes a close second."

"Follow my lead and you can have a boat load of the stuff."

"Yes, Sir," he replied with a mock salute and a wobble that nearly saw him fall from his horse.

Jack led the way through the town, directly and purposefully to the door of the revenue office, dismounting a few yards down the street, so as to use the shadow of his horse, to hide his identity. There was still activity in the office. A ship's captain could be seen from the open door, registering his cargo, while two of Winter's men warmed themselves by the stove.

"We'll visit when Mr Winter is less busy... He might even be stupid enough to visit us!" Once more Jack grinned, worrying Weaverton further. "While we wait, I'll buy you a drink."

"That is a notion to celebrate," Weaverton replied, refitting the cork to his flask, to conserve his supply. "Shall we try this one?"

"No... An old friend once taught me that you can judge a man by his choice of ale house, just as you can judge an ale house by the men that drink there."

"Sounds like Peter."

"It was," Jack agreed. "We're looking for a dark ally and an unmarked house."

"And a knife in the ribs," Weaverton grumbled as they continued on, to a narrow ally, barely noticeable off the main street.

The sound of drunkenness resonating down the unlit ally, marked the ale house as clearly as any sign could. As two men ahead of them opened the door, it shone enough light on the rough stone path, outside, and enough to see a sailor laying in a pool of his own vomit, barely conscious.

"Quality establishment," Weaverton commented dryly.

"No more posh gentleman's clubs for you, Mr Jones," Jack said, by means of a reminder of his new identity.

"Well it's a club of some sorts," Weaverton warned him as every pair of eyes in the room quickly fixed upon them, the rowdy noise of drunken men almost instantly quietening to a whisper.

"Sorry about the intrusion, gentlemen... My friend here seems to have misplaced his ship," Jack announced through the nerve-racking silence. The silence continued. The men looked at each other, confused by their presence in what wasn't actually an officially public house. "Do you know the worst of it?" Jack laughed, despite the icy silence. "He's the bloody Captain."

"Alright," a rugged man, in his thirties laughed, considering them both too drunk to know what they were doing or saying. "Tell us the name of your ship and we'll direct you on your way."

"That's the spirit... It's the Thorn." As the last word left his mouth, he drew both pistols, pointing them directly at the two most prominent men in the room. Weaverton followed his lead, pulling a light pistol from the lining of his jacket.

"You see, this is Romulus Jones; your new Captain. I assume I am talking to the crew of the Thorn?"

"You won't be Captaining anything, where you're going," a strong voice boomed from the back of the room. The crowd opened to reveal a short, but stout man, standing with a pistol in one hand and a short bladed cutlass in the other.

"First mate. Am I right?" Weaverton said cheerfully, as if it were a polite conversation, about the weather. "Loyal lap dog," he added to the groans and sniggers of the men watching.

"Don't just stand there, jump to it. Get them done in," the stout man ordered, whilst focusing his vision on the pistol trained on him.

"That's your problem, you see. They want to know what their new Captain has to offer." Jack's eyes were flitting around the room, expecting at any moment for another pistol, or a blade to be pulled.

In contrast, Weaverton stepped forwards as if he were addressing a knitting club. "Unfortunately, Sir, I'm having a bit of a rearrangement. The first mate is now Mr Rib Bone Jack," Weaverton boldly gestured towards Jack, as he spoke the name that had become so notorious across England and beyond. "I'm sure we can find you something useful to do in the galley." Two men openly dared to laugh at the statement; a sign that Jack's deduction was right and that the crew were indeed ready to mutiny.

Weaverton turned his back on them for a few seconds, considering the short, hurried briefing Jack had given him as they walked down the alley. Turning his back was an act of theatre; a demonstration that he wasn't afraid of them. He casually stepped up onto a rough table and looked down upon the room of desperate men. "I offer you your pride back," he eventually exclaimed. "There are those in the world that consider smuggling an honest profession. Rebalancing the scales in favour of the many, but what you are, what you've become is something worse, something unspeakable. Traitors. Servants of the enemy."

"What would you have us do? We'll swing for a cargo of Irish whisky, just the same as we'll swing for a few frogs," a youngster, the worse for drink, interrupted.

"It's true," Jack replied from the floor. "You'll swing, just the same, but for the frogs, your families will be burnt out of their houses and beaten in the streets... Even the lowliest thief goes to his death with just a hint of pride, knowing he was dying for the crime of feeding his family, but you lot, you will swing with a brand of shame so dark that your wives and children won't dare speak your accursed name."

The first mate was becoming more agitated. Looking around the room, scowling at the men for even listening. "I don't know what you think we are, posh boy," he snarled, pointing his pistol straight at Weaverton. "None of us are swinging. Our Captain Magnusson has always kept us safe."

"Magnusson? That's a good old Welsh name," Weaverton laughed facetiously.

"Where's he from? One of them shitty little countries with their heads up Napoleon's arse?" Jack asked, inspiring the first mate to redirect his pistol at him.

"I heard Rib Bone Jack was dead. Done in by the Spanish," the drunken youngster called out.

"I heard it was the French," another man said.

"It was the Spanish that done this," he relied, re-holstering the pistol in his right hand and pulling his trouser leg up high enough to expose the scarring on his leg. "And the French had a good go," he added, pulling his shirt open to expose the hook scar across his ribs, which so clearly identified him. "But I'm not that bloody easy to kill."

The crew began to whisper amongst themselves, ignoring both the first mate and the fact that they were at gunpoint. Jack and Weaverton shared a nervous glance.

"Damn your hides," the first mate bellowed, as he hurried, backwards, towards the kitchen door. His retreat was all the convincing the doubters needed.

"We'll still be bringing in the grog?" a man with a heavy beard asked from the table near the window.

"And whatever else South Wales is of a mind to buy from us. Just not festering Frenchmen!"

The bearded man drew his pistol at speed, prompting both Jack and Weaverton to turn there guns towards him, but before they could fire, he had fired his pistol through the window. "We can't have him running to Captain, can we!" he said, casually replacing his pistol in his belt.

"What's your name, man?" Weaverton asked, as both he and Jack lowered their pistols.

"Percival Plowright, Captain," he replied, with a boldness not befitting an ordinary crewman. "Known to some as Purse."

"That's probably the finest pistol shot I've ever seen, Mr Plowright," Weaverton replied, as he walked to the window to see the dead body of the first mate, lying on the stones, outside. Shot cleanly from his horse, at a gallop.

"I was aiming for the horse, Captain," he replied, without a hint of humour.

Chapter 17

For Charlie, the lone ride in the darkness was well needed thinking time. As he rode across the uneven, rocky ground, which was far from safe riding, even in daylight, he considered the path his life had taken. He had signed himself up to a straightforward life; the life of an English officer, with a wife and family. The enemy on the opposite side of the battlefield, friends and allies by his side. That was how it had been told to him, when he was just a child, and it inspired him.

The reality had proved so different. The loyalties of not just the soldiers and men of power, around him, but also his own family, were seldom that clear. He had seen betrayal that no man should, and in the process his allegiances had been tested further than seemed fair or right.

He continued through the darkness, wondering what his daughter would look like now, if he could but see her. If his wife was loyal to his memory, or if she considered their severed relationship freedom to move on. The first sight of the sea, as he reached the top of a particularly rocky hill, reminded him of the day he put them both on the ship; his sense of betrayal so strong that he could barely speak to them.

With the lights of Tenby to his left and a coastal track ahead of him, he made a conscious decision to keep his wits about him and dispel thoughts of the past from his mind. He followed the track to his right, dismounting to guide his horse away from the ever steeper drop along the narrow, rocky path. Without warning, his horse would stumble, slipping on the loose rocks of the seldom used path, each time panicking for a moment, before calming again as he whispered softly to it.

In the distance, a rocky mass seemed to rise from the sea, considerably higher than the level he was standing at. It was only visible as an imposing silhouette, but despite the sketchy instructions the Welsh farmer had given him, it was unmistakable.

He watched the landscape behind it hawkishly, whilst listening for the laughter and hilarity that he associated with a soldiers camp. Despite only being about three miles out of town, the land was arid and useless. Nothing edible grew there, not for man nor beast, and as a result, the whole area appeared uninhabited. Only occasionally, a flickering light could be seen from the sparsely dotted cottages and livestock holdings, further in land, but nothing close to the area directly behind the rock formation, which his informant was sure to be the camp.

The occasional weeds, growing on the narrowing path became gradually more plentiful as he got further from the town, indicating to him that the whole idea might just be the work of loose tongues and the over active imaginations of the locals.

Suddenly, without warning, the path vanished. Once more his horse panicked, but this time it was with good reason, and may well have saved Charlie from serious injury. In the faint light, much of which was shining off the sea, he could just make out the sudden, steep rockfall, which had taken out about ten yards of the path.

For a couple of minutes he considered turning back. It was only the imposing rock formation that kept him from giving up entirely. It seemed to protrude out, into the sea. His curiosity for what might be behind it was the one thing that made him doubt what was the only sensible decision; to turn back. The tree saplings growing on the stony surface ahead of him, suggested that it had been done for some time. "Bloody convenient," he muttered to himself, as he realised the loss of the path had isolated that stretch of the coastline from human activity.

As the wind began to pick up with an impending storm, which reduced the light further, Charlie continued back for almost half a mile, to the point where the path led inland. An unusually healthy patch of grass nestled in a tiny clearing amongst the otherwise thorn tree dominated landscape. "Wait here, old son," he whispered, patting his horse on the neck. He tied him loosely, to allow him to graze. "No place for horses, where I'm going," he muttered, as if he expected the animal to argue.

It was an application of common sense that led Charlie to the usable road, the treacherous terrain being so extreme that there were few alternatives. He scrambled through a hundred yards or more, of rocky hillside, smothered in thorn bushes and brambles, before coming out onto a heavily used track.

The smell of fresh horse droppings gave away the fact that riders had recently passed, despite the darkness. He felt on the ground, for the dusty, uneven texture of the stones and soil, indicating the recent disturbance.

As soon as the bushes started to clear, he could see the light glowing from an area at the base of the rocks, in the distance. It could have been drovers, gypsies, or just rough sleepers, but somehow, with all that was going on, that didn't seem likely.

He walked boldly and upright, down the centre of the path, not being prepared to surrender an ounce of pride by skulking in the bushes.

Only a couple of hundred yards from the camp, he continued walking without slowing his pace. Even as the track took its last meander, he held his pace. He saw a tiny glowing light on the track ahead; the glow from the sentry's smouldering pipe, marked the point of no return.

"Hello, in the camp," Charlie called, only then slowing his step. "Don't shoot if you know what's good for you."

The hurried clicking of a hammer, accompanied the bumbling rustlings of an unprepared man. "Name yourself," the guard demanded, in a strong Welsh accent.

"Captain Charles Halfbasket," Charlie replied, still steadily pacing forwards.

"Halt," the guard demanded, stepping into full view with his musket trained on Charlie.

"I think you'll find your Major is expecting me," he replied calmly, whilst continuing forwards. "A slippery trigger will kill you, just as sure as it'll kill me."

Now only yards away, the guard was panicking. His hand began to shake as he brought the musket back to his shoulder, having finally made the decision to fire.

"Stand down, man," the commanding voice of Major Elmshall ordered from the track behind him.

Elmshall stood as a shadow, behind the guard. "Captain Halfbasket, anyone would think you wanted to get killed," he said smugly, guiding Charlie to the camp.

Chapter 18

"There she sits, Captain," Owain Lark said, pointing out to a dusky silhouette of a ship, anchored in full view, beyond the harbour.

"Bloody hell, you're pushing you luck, aren't you," Jack said, amazed that the notorious smugglers ship was on full display.

"We've never been given any reason to hide," Lark replied. "Not until now."

"Oh, I plan to give you plenty of reasons to hide," Jack said, reaching over the wall to see what was below.

"Tunnels, Mr. To the merchants and tradesmen, straight from dock." Lark spoke proudly of the town, in his strong Welsh accent. "My father helped build them."

"Does one of them happen to lead to the revenue pound?" Jack said with a smirk.

"Six inches of English oak says you won't get a whore's spit of the stuff," Lark replied, with concern in his voice. "It's been half an hour since we met you two, and you're already making pirates of us."

"Like the lad said; you'll pay the same price," Weaverton said smugly. "And you won't be lining the frog's pockets, only our own."

"Where would we shift if. We'd all be dead men as soon as we set foot on dry land."

"There's an alehouse in Norfolk. They will shift all we can get," Jack said as he ushered the eighteen men behind a wooden building, out of view.

"Bloody Norfolk!" an Irishman exclaimed.

"No Frenchies there and a bloody sight less chance of running into English soldiers," Jack argued.

"I thought he was meant to be the Captain," Lark muttered, as he led the way down a wooden ladder, to their moored rowing boat.

As Lark led the others down to the moored boat, Weaverton held Jack back. "Don't think I don't know what you're up to... I've had more to do with the old Major's scheming that you, don't forget."

"The way I see it, King George still owes me a pretty penny for that throne he still sits on."

"No... Like I said, I've seen more of the Major than most, and you are the nearest to him I've seen." Weaverton continued to smile, every word he spoke was said in a round about way, as if it was of no importance, such was his view of all things, since what he saw as a betrayal by the system. "An attack on the King's revenue is an attack on the king himself. You plan to cause enough trouble to bring soldiers, without a word of Frenchmen."

"Are you with me?" Jack asked in a contrastingly serious tone.

"I've no where else to be... Will they be properly compensated?" he asked with genuine concern for the men, who had been under his command for all of half an hour.

"There's a good purse for whatever lands, and a harbour more or less free of the revenue."

"Sounds like we're business partners," Weaverton said, grabbing Jack's hand to shake.

"You've got to win your ship, yet, and your crew."

"What do you mean," Weaverton said with genuine confusion. "They've been waiting for this, you said it yourself."

"Doesn't mean they won't let you deal with the Captain... Test your metal."

"Might be a problem with that," Weaverton muttered sheepishly, pulling his jacket to one side to expose an empty scabbard, where his sword once proudly hung.

"Where'd you loose that?"

"Irish whiskey doesn't buy itself, you know," he argued.

"You sold it?" Jack exclaimed with dismay.

"No. It was more a lone, until the present financial clouds have past."

"Are you coming," Lark called, loudly enough to attract the attention of a pair of drinkers on the far side of the street.

"Looks like you still need nanny," Jack grumbled as he followed Weaverton down the ladder.

As they rowed, they began to sing; not just one song but two or three, all merging into one, slurred from drunkenness and completely without coordination. A giant Russian rowed with two oars, at the bow, singing in his native tongue, just adding to the confusion. The efforts of every other man working a single oar, seemed half-hearted in comparison.

Only the would be Captain Jones avoided rowing. His privileged background made this acceptable to him, but more than that, it made him more a natural leader than Jack would ever be, and they both knew it.

The crew seemed excited. All the burning resentment that had built up over time, particularly towards the French crewmen, had been brought to a head with ease.

As the boat drew in close to the Thorn, a Frenchman reached over the side, drawing them in with a long pole. "That's not right, flying the Jack, with French on board," Weaverton complained, taking that affront more seriously than anything else that had taken place that evening.

"Captain... I mean Magnusson says it helps us to go unnoticed, Sir," Lark explained.

The Frenchman muttered words in his own tongue as he pulled the boat tight to the ship's hull; words which the crew knew were more likely than not, insulting. One man stood up and gripped the pole, yanking it firmly, while Nicolasher, the giant Russian swung an oar, cracking the Frenchman's skull and delivering death instantly with his great strength. As if it had been practised, the man on the end of the pole yanked it at the perfect moment to deliver the body to the boat without a splash.

The men allowed themselves a small cheer, for the death of the first of their French shipmates; a noise that was in no way out of place amongst the drunken chants and ramblings, which was in keeping with their usual return to the ship.

The crew scrambled up the side of the ship, like rats, and without a word of an order. Whatever the long term held for his captaincy, Weaverton knew then that the fate of those Frenchmen was entirely out of his hands.

Jack was the last on Deck, his weak leg found climbing the thick rope net, difficult. By the time he was on deck every part of the deck was occupied. A sudden silence came over the crew as they waited. "Jean," the Irishman eventually called, focusing his attention and a pistol, on the small door, down to the lower deck.

"What do you want, you drunken bastard," a strong French accent replied, amidst the giggling of drunken women.

"Best grog, proper Irish Grog." As footsteps could be heard below, the youngster, who had been so keen to speak his mind earlier in the night, stepped forwards, putting his hand on the Irishman's pistol, whilst gleefully waving his knife.

"Grog or none, you still owe me," the Frenchman grumbled as he appeared in the little doorway. For just a moment he stopped, looking around the deck as the realisation came to him that something was wrong. Before he could make any sort of move, the youngster pounced from behind the door, like a cat with a mouse, slitting his throat with little effort.

Jack stepped forwards, drawing a pistol, but Weaverton grabbed his shoulder. "This is theirs... Sometimes a man needs to break his own shackles."

"Captain Magnusson," Lark called loudly, as he stood beside the Irishman, facing the deck door.

"Get some clothes on, you dogs," Magnusson growled at the two remaining Frenchmen. As he appeared in the doorway, he stood, highlighted by the lamp he was carrying in his left hand. In his right hand, he held a cocked pistol; one of a row of four, which he wore around his waist.

"So you've finally found the salt, Mr Lark," he snarled through the full beard that gave him the appearance of a bear.

Lark was visibly shaken by the sight of his Captain, directing a pistol at him. "We've decided, Captain. We want the Thorn to be free of Frenchmen."

"I can see that," Magnusson growled, stepping over the feet of the dead man to make room for the other two Frenchmen to join him, on Deck. "Who are these bastards," he demanded, pointing at Jack and Weaverton with his pistol.

"What's the accent, Captain?" Jack asked, being keen to associate Magnusson with the enemy, in the eyes of the crew.

"I'll ask the questions, aboard my bloody ship," he snapped, directing his pistol at Jack. The two stared at each other as the rain began to lash in heavy pulses, driven by the increasing wind.

"You want my ship; you can fight for it," Magnusson exclaimed, placing his pistol back in the spectacular belt of pistols and drawing an equally showy wide bladed sword.

Weaverton holstered his pistol and pulled open his jacket to demonstrate his lack of a sword. "Lost to an earlier engagement," he said proudly, the less admirable truth not causing him any concern.

"A Captain's first job is to make sure his men are equipped for the job ahead, what ever it may be, and you, you useless horse shit, dare to ask the men you would have follow you, for a sword." As the rain ran down Magnusson's face, soaking his beard, Jack could see the reason his men were so afraid of him. He had an imposing presence that made a man instinctively fear him. "Shoot any man that dares to arm their new Captain," Magnusson instructed the two Frenchmen, who in turn brought their muskets to their shoulder.

"And I will shoot them both dead, one breath later," Jack assured him, training his pistols on the Frenchmen.

Weaverton looked around. He looked at the crew, who had listened to Magnusson's words with an open mind. He knew winning the fight was only half of it; he had to win their respect to ever captain that ship.

"For two pins I'd shoot you where you stand. Plenty good enough for a Frenchman's lacky, but you see I've business back in Tenby, and there's already been one more shot fired tonight, than I'd planned, when your first mate bit the cobbles... Don't want to make your friend Winter, nervous." As he spoke, he looked over various pieces of equipment laying in a disorganised heap, on the deck beside him. "What's the meaning of this, Mr Lark?" he asked sternly. "A man could fall overboard on this."

He picked up a pulley block, on a short rope and began to swing it in a threatening manner.

Magnusson grinned at the feeble threat, taking a couple of mock lunges, just to test his reactions. "Is this your choice of Captain?" he growled angrily, pulling the sword back to deliver such a blow that would cut through almost anything put in its way. Every man present held his breath, gasped or winced at the impending death of their new Captain.

As Magnusson's sword reached its furthest point from him, Weaverton dropped from the jacket sleeve of his left hand, a narrow bladed dagger and caught it as it slipped past his hand, at the same moment he dropped the pulley block, and lunged forwards, grabbing at Magnusson's sword arm as he thrust the dagger under his ribs.

Weaverton didn't immediately allow Magnusson to drop to the floor. He held him up by the dagger and brought him close, as the crew cheered and goaded around him. "I would have gladly fought you in an honourable manner," Weaverton said calmly as Magnusson's blood poured down his hand. "The trouble is, the French blaggards you've been delivering to our shores took my honourable name from me, so there really wasn't a lot of point." Magnusson looked back through angry eyes, which slowly lost their fire, as the life drained from his body.

"I'll be keeping that belt, Mr Lark," Weaverton ordered as he eventually allowed Magnusson's corpse to drop to the deck.

"Captain," he exclaimed as he delivered a full military style salute. "What about the frogs, Captain?" He asked of the two Frenchmen, who had surrendered the moment Magnusson was stabbed.

"Clap em in irons, Mr Lark. We've a lot of grog to shift tonight. They can earn the air they breath."

"What about these, Captain," Purse Ploughwright asked as he pushed two frightened, snivelling whores through the deck hatch.

"Sorry ladies. You're no good to any of us... Tainted by Frenchmen!" he joked, playing for the crowd. "Besides, these lads are way too pissed... You'll be safely delivered to shore, once our business here is done," he said cheerfully.

Jack stood back and watched as his old friend took his place as Captain. He laughed to himself, considering the arrogant aristocrat Weaverton once was, yet he was also a man with no place he had ever truly fitted, until that moment.

"Mr Lark, have that flag removed," the newly appointed Captain instructed as he walked the rain lashed deck, as if it were a summers day. "We have no right to sail by that flag."

"Aye, Captain," Lark replied hesitantly. "But what are we to fly, Captain. Surely we have to fly some sort of colours."

Jack grinned at the statement. "Do you remember my old friend, Drum?" he asked. "Do you remember how we broke him out of the hangman's cart."

"The flag!.. I wasn't there, but I've heard the bloody story enough times," Weaverton said with an air of joy. "Ladies. Before you go, could I ask one last thing of you," he asked of the whores as they were being eagerly escorted below decks by two of the crew.

"That flag's definitely more French than English," Lark complained, without a hint of humour, as he handed a pair of knee length, frilly bloomers to the youngest of the crew, to replace the union Jack.

"Take her to harbour, Mr Lark," Weaverton ordered with drunken joy and restored pride in equal measure.

Chapter 19

Charlie had sat away from the fire, beneath an overhanging rock, which the Frenchmen had avoided, due to its likelihood of falling in the storm. In doing so he was the only man present not to be lashed by the heavy squall, which was battering the South Wales coast. He was secluded there, almost out of sight of Elmshall's mainly Frenchmen, and, as such, if he put his mind to it, he could forget that he was in league with the enemy.

He polished his rifle again and again, not just in preparation for the job it must do, but as a matter of therapy; something he had done thousands of times before, something that felt normal.

On the rock beside him, he had laid a letter with two locks of hair, fixed to it with sealing wax. He was keeping it close now, to be sure he knew what was at stake, and to be sure he kept his nerve.

"They'll be just as dead if that rock flattens you," Elmshall said merrily as he approached.

"If I'm half frozen in this bloody rain, I might miss... The man I must kill won't wait about for a second shot." Charlie didn't look up or slow his polishing. He couldn't face Elmshall. It was all he could do not to kill him on the spot, but if he did, he knew it would be the death of his wife and daughter, in America.

"You seem sure he's all that needs to be done... You know it's the success of my mission that keeps your family alive."

"I assume the servants are already salted in a barrel!"

"A necessary precaution, I'm sure you understand."

Charlie paused, considering the terror his wife and child were enduring. "With Bones dead, the rest will leave you to it... Nobody else needs to die," Charlie insisted, at last looking up at Elmshall.

"Best you get to it then, Captain. We both know where he is tonight. By morning he could be anywhere."

Charlie got up without speaking, knowing there was no way of delaying any further, what he had to do. He carefully folded the letter, deliberately turning his back on Elmshall as a matter of disrespect. "Before you go, Major," he said as Elmshall walked back towards the large fire, surrounded by Frenchmen. Elmshall stopped, but didn't turn around. "Understand that I will be doing the honourable thing, once I know my family are safe, but if they are not, the entire French army won't keep you alive."

Elmshall smiled and continued walking, delighted by the misery he was inflicting on Charlie's tormented soul. Charlie began to walk from the camp, turning his face against the rain and against the sight of the Frenchmen, only feet away from him.

"Captain. You might want to wait a minute, and meet our other guests," Elmshall called to him, as the sound of hooves on the track and the distressed whimpering of crying women reached them.

Charlie stopped in his tracks, watching with dread as the approaching riders came into view. One Frenchman rode victoriously, ahead, while a second walked a horse with two battered women on its back; Camilla and Estelle.

"Call it a fall back plan, in case you miss," Elmshall said smugly.

Camilla wiped her face with the sleeve of her ripped dress, her hands having been tied tightly in front of her. "Charlie," she gasped with horror. "All the time, Jack was right."

Charlie couldn't look at her. "You need to pray I don't miss, now," he said in disgust, before continuing on his way.

Chapter 20

The Thorn drifted into harbour with an atmospheric silence. Every man had his orders, and, drunk or not, they set to them with a new focus, the divisions caused by their French passengers having died with Magnusson.

There was the odd labourer and sailor out and about in the town, but the continuing icy rain meant that no man lingered longer than his journey home demanded. To most men of Tenby, the Thorn was known, not as a vessel you would talk about openly, but in whispers; most only ever having seen it as a silhouette on the horizon, anchored while its illicit cargo was rowed ashore.

Jack gave a nod to the man he was now obliged to call Captain Jones, before climbing down a rope, on the side of the ship, leaping onto the deck of a moored boat as the Thorn drifted past. It only bought him a couple of minutes head start, but he considered it the edge he needed.

"That's not a sight you see every day, boy," a drunken labourer slurred as Jack hurried past him.

"I'll tell you another... As much grog as you can drink for a half an hour's work. Just join my friends at the mooring." Jack spoke as he passed, not slowing his pace.

"Would there be tax on that, boyo?" the man asked as Jack disappeared into the darkness.

Though it was late, Jack had no doubt that Winter would still be found at the revenue office. Too much had gone on that day for any man to just lock up and go home.

He walked boldly, as he turned the corner of the revenue building. He found half measures and caution had seldom served him well, where as inappropriate confidence seemed to wrong foot his opponents. He pushed the door open as if he lived there, causing the two men, standing just inside the doorway, to look around. They didn't seem to instantly recognise him, as if they were expecting someone else. Only as Jack drew a pistol in his right hand, did they draw back against the narrow wall at the back.

As Jack continued into the room, Winter sat at his paper strewn desk. "I've been expecting you for some hours, Mr Bones. Whatever has kept you."

"Put your hands in the open," Jack demanded, as Winter sat with his hands behind the desk.

"Are you men armed?" Winter asked, ignoring Jack's instruction. One of the men pulled back his jacket to expose a pistol, wedged in his belt. His failure to speak and the general look about him told Jack that these were Elmshall's Frenchmen.

"You know I'm not alone, don't you?" Jack said, as he drew a broken shear blade from his belt.

"You should know not to trust your friends," Winter said smugly as his hand moved towards the desk draw.

Jack studied the two men, who were awaiting their orders from Winter. The nearest of the two stared back with a hawkish glare. He stood rigid, ready to fight. He was undoubtedly a seasoned soldier, and one with a taste for killing.

The second man was quite different. He stood, wedging himself in the corner, almost shrinking as Jack looked at him. He knew fear, that much was clear. If he drew his pistol at all, there was a good chance he'd miss.

The slight squeak of Winter's desk draw was all it took. As Winter fumbled in the draw, Jack lunged forwards, hurling the shear blade at the first man's chest and slamming into the desk with his thigh at the same time, trapping Winter's hand briefly. He grabbed Winter by the collar and dragged him across the desk, before he could lay a hand on the pistol in the draw.

As his friend propped himself against the back wall, clutching the handle of the shearing blade, the second man hurriedly put his hands up, without making any attempt at drawing his pistol.

"Where's the keys?" Jack demanded of Winter, who was now partially stretched across his desk, with his head pressed against the wood.

"Desk," Winter mumbled, his voice muffled by Jack's hand pressing hard on the side of his face.

Jack continuously watched the two Frenchmen as he pushed Winter from the desk, onto the floor. The injured man had slid onto the floor; the blood pouring through his fingers and his face filling with terror, as the colour left him from the loss of blood.

Jack fumbled awkwardly in the desk draw, for the keys; first removing Winter's pistol and placing it in his belt as an extra shot, should he need it.

"You'll never make it out of Wales, you bloody fool," Winter grumbled, clutching his skinned and bruised hand. "You'll not even get out of Tenby."

"Now why might that be?" Jack asked, sensing a reason for the statement. Winter smiled slightly, in response as Jack looked out of the window, nervously.

"Your pistol, and his," Jack demanded, pointing at the pistol in the second man's belt with the assumption that he didn't have good English.

The Frenchman slowly placed both pistols on the floor, in front of him, only ever holding them with two fingers, in fear of giving Jack reason to shoot him.

"Come here," Jack demanded, beckoning him towards him. "I'll need your coat," the man nodded obligingly, as he dragged off the heavy fisherman's coat, briefly looking back to his friend, who stared back at him through dead eyes.

Jack took his Jacket off and handed it to him. "About your size... Exchange is no robbery." The Frenchman panicked.

"No, no," he pleaded, as Jack thrust it in his hands.

"Put it on."

"No. Please," The Frenchman begged, pushing the jacket back.

Jack cocked his pistol and put it to his head, until he dragged the jacket over his shaking arms. "Run," he ordered, pulling the door open as he slung the Frenchman into the street, before slamming the door closed behind him. Before Jack could get the key in the lock, a shot rang out, dropping the Frenchman in a heap about five yards from the door.

"A bloody good Jacket, that was," Jack complained, as he refocused his attention on Winter. "Walk time," he said as he gestured for him to lead the way through the door at the back. "So, do you feel like telling me why you killed Davis?" Jack asked as they descended the long stone flight of stairs.

"That was Halls... I wouldn't."

"He was in your care. Just because it wasn't your hand that did it, doesn't make you any the less his killer," Jack interrupted angrily. "Was he too honest for you?"

"He knew about the smuggling, everyone did. It was when he found out about the French, that he began to talk to people."

"And the poor sods that hung for it? I suppose you were nothing to do with that either?"

"They would have hung anyway. They were caught fair and square."

"So what made them different to Elmshall and all the other stuff coming into South Wales?"

"A percentage, Mr Bones... There's unimaginable money to be had, if you were of a mind." Despite the despicable crimes he had just admitted to, he spoke with a stomach churning air of superiority.

"On that we can agree," Jack said, as they walked past the vast hoards of goods, stacked to the brick-weave ceiling. "That's why we're taking the bloody lot."

"Bloody hell, Jack. We were about to blow the thing," Weaverton complained as Jack pulled open the vast oak door.

"Don't take the powder. We're going to need that," Jack said with a grin at the sight of three barrels of powder, which had been stood against the door.

"Mr Winter, Sir!" the giant Russian boomed, performing a military salute.

"We've grabbed three men off the street, at gunpoint of course, Sir. Just like you ordered," Lark bellowed, deliberately loudly. "I'd just like to say, on behalf of the crew, how grateful we all are for this opportunity you've organised for us." As the crew and the three townsmen filed past, every man saluted or doffed his hat to Winter, while Jack discretely jabbed him in the ribs with his knife every time he attempted to speak.

"You see, we're of the same mind. It really doesn't matter what a man hangs for, so long as he hangs," Jack explained as boxes and barrels filed past.

"Did you want the grog on first, Sir," one of the townsmen asked him, as he passed with a barrel on his shoulder. "I doubt there's room for it all."

Winter hung his head, Jack's blade being pressed so hard as to be drawing blood. "You see, you are going to face the people of Tenby; the families of the men you have hung for doing a little bit of what you've done a lot of. They're going to watch you hang."

"It'll not come to that. Not while Halls is out there."

"You're no more use to him. The worst he'll do is slit your throat before you blab," Jack whispered, once he was sure each of the three men had seen enough to testify, before pushing him out onto the wooden jetty. "Come now, boss. We must get you to safety," Jack called out, as he took Winter out of sight of the crew and pushed him into a small rowing boat.

Before Winter could protest a word, Jack hit him hard, around the back of the head, with an oar, before untying the boat, to drift.

He climbed the short ladder, up to street level, while the crew continued to load the ship. There was activity around the revenue office, but only a handful of men, inspecting the corpse of the shot stranger. The people of Tenby had become so accustomed to turning a blind eye, particularly to matters relating to the revenue, that the fatal shot had only inspired most people to close their curtains.

He stood, watch in the shadows, considering his next move. He had so craved the capture of Elmshall for the murder of the young woman in Great Yarmouth, but he had so much more to lose now, since he and Peter had vowed to catch him. He could sail on the Thorn and send for Camilla to join him, or he could collect her from Cravith and meet the Thorn in Norfolk. In either case, he was offering her an outlaw's life.

"Mind you don't strain yourself with those heavy pistols," Weaverton said dryly.

"How's it going?"

"We're going to sit low in the water, and we'll be leaving a good lot behind, even then," Weaverton said, before swigging on his freshly filled hip flask.

"We won't leave them a drop... Blow the bloody lot up. Give em something to talk about; ample reason to send soldiers!"

Weaverton pointed across the street. "Someone means business." Two figures, one significantly larger than the other, were walking briskly towards them.

"Revenue men?" Jack suggested, drawing a pistol.

"No... Bible pushers!" Weaverton said in amazement as Bart Baker and Lord Cravith walked from the darkness.

"There are men assembling on the back streets. Looks like the revenue," Cravith puffed, his breath short from his having run across town.

"Don't worry... By the time they find the guts, we'll be done," Jack said, confident in their cowardice.

"They've got Camilla, Jack... and Estelle," Bart said, between gasps, eventually finding the breath to speak.

"Who? The bloody revenue?"

"No, Elmshall," Bart said desperately.

"How?"

"They left two men behind, just waiting for their chance," Cravith explained with an air of apology.

"Just like that?"

"The livestock had been scattered. Those who were able began to round them up... The ladies volunteered."

"And you let them!" Jack snapped angrily.

"I didn't see you waiting around to protect her," Cravith snarled back; his Welsh accent all the stronger for his anger.

"Maybe you should just shoot each other and save Elmshall the trouble," Weaverton suggested merrily, as if it was a worthwhile option.

"Where are they? Did Charlie come back to the village?"

"No sign of Captain Halfbasket, but we think we know where the camp is." Cravith looked past him as he spoke, to the ship being hastily loaded. "Is that the Thorn?"

"Beautiful, ain't she," Weaverton said proudly.

"Are they?.." he asked, at the sight of the bloomers blowing in the wind, on the flag staff.

"Yes, they are!" Weaverton replied with equal pride.

"Remember. Sky high," Jack said as he turned to Weaverton, making an exploding gesture with his hands. "My family will be waiting for you in Norfolk, even if I'm delayed," Jack assured him, as they shook hands as the friends that they only sometimes were.

"You won't be delayed, but best of luck to you, anyway," he said as he turned and vanished into the darkness, to rejoin his crew.

"Is this all we are?" Jack asked, as they followed the shadows away from the harbour, to avoid being spotted by the revenue men and volunteers, gathering in the next street.

"My people can do no more," Cravith insisted. "They're shepherds and labourers, not..."

"They are admirable people," Bart interrupted, seeing that Cravith was beginning to get worked up.

"They are indeed. None the less we need to get an edge on the bastard." Jack spoke vaguely, as if he was thinking out loud, rather than talking specifically to them. "We need to get back to my horse. If we do away with Elmshall, the frogs will disappear like the morning dew."

"How do you plan to do that? He leads from the back, you said that yourself," Cravith argued.

"I plan to challenge him to a duel... I don't believe he could help but accept."

"That's because he knows he'll win... Bloody hell, Jack he's the best duellist in England," Bart complained angrily.

"Bloody good thing we're in Wales, then!"

"I can't fix a shot through the heart. There's no bandages for that!" Bart whined insistently. "You're not even that fast with a pistol, and he never misses. Through the heart, every time. You've heard Horry's stories."

"Just stories! If you two can get to the women, I'll deal with Elmshall."

Chapter 21

Charlie walked his horse into Elmshall's camp, as a troubled man. He had crossed a line from which he could not return, and he knew there was more to come. The first sight he saw as he entered the camp was Camilla and Estelle, tied back to back, close the camp fire. Two of the Frenchmen were leering and goading them. He noticed that the front of Camilla's dress had been torn further than it was when he left the camp, now barely covering her breasts.

"Major, can I ask that some gentlemanly behaviour be extended towards the women," he said loudly, hoping that even if Elmshall didn't act on his request, the men might.

"No Gentlemen here, is there men?" Elmshall boomed to the cheers of the half a dozen or so men who were still conscious. In response, a vile looking man with ragged, greasy hair and blackened teeth spat a mouthful of the rabbit leg he was chewing at Estelle, just to prove a point. "Have you news for me, Captain?"

"I believe I got him," Charlie said sombrely, looking at the ground in his own disgrace, now more unable to face Camilla than ever.

"You believe?.. Either he's dead or he's not," Elmshall snapped.

"The man I shot is dead, and it looked like him, but."

"But what, Captain?"

Charlie dared to look across at Camilla, who was glaring back at him. "Bastard," she shouted, bursting into tears as she guessed what was being discussed. "He was your friend," she snivelled, kicking her feet in the dirt in a hopeless attempt to loosen the ropes around them. The Frenchman nearest to her, prodded her arm with a stick, tearing her sleeve.

"It was just too easy," Charlie said, walking away from Elmshall, towards the Frenchman.

"What's wrong, Captain, you wanting this one for your self?" the Frenchman jeered in his poor English.

Charlie picked up the same piece of stick and began to prod the Frenchman; his anger rapidly escalating out of control. "What's wrong, froggy, don't you like it?" He began to thrash the man as he blundered and scrambled away, never quite managing to get back onto his feet.

Far from stopping the beating, Elmshall watched; his face filled with joy as the beating appealed to his cruel nature. "Fight back man," he called, as the stick in Charlie's hand broke again and again, until there was no more than six inches left. Only then did the Frenchman begin to fight back. In stead of cowering, as he had been, he picked up a fist sized rock and began to swing it towards Charlie, in the palm of his hand. With the first swing, Charlie stepped back, dodging the impact by a couple of inches. Without a pause, the Frenchman swung it back; confident that he had the upper hand. With the third swing, Charlie blocked the rock with his left hand and rammed the short piece of stick forwards, jamming it under the man's chin with all the force he could muster.

"Like a true gentleman," Elmshall boomed sarcastically, laughing loudly to bring an end to the fight before Charlie finished the job. Charlie looked back at him, briefly, whilst still holding the stick, which was wedged a short distance into the flesh of the man's chin. He looked across at the women, who were watching, not in horror, but in hope.

All but one particularly drunken man was now awake and watching, not worried for their comrade, but entertained by his misfortune.

The man stood with his heels off the ground in a futile hope of relieving the pressure from the stick, which was now running blood onto Charlie's hand. He looked into Charlie's eyes, petrified by the anger he saw there. "Nobody touches the women," Charlie called across the camp, before throwing the stick on the ground, frustrated to be releasing the man who was in his eyes, still the enemy.

"Very good, Captain... It's was probably a good choice not to give in to your more primitive instincts, though. That's the man I'll be sending to with word of my well-being and your good behaviour... There is, as you know, a dispatch that will be sent to the home of your family, should that message not be reported." Elmshall was smug with his threat, toying with Charlie like a cat with a mouse.

"What more do you want from me?" Charlie demanded, less defiantly and more in a state of desperation, like a man with somewhere he needed to be.

"Everything you know... The Sparesons. Who they are. Where they are to be found. What they are doing... Call it an act of good will," he said with a sugary falseness that made Charlie want to kill him all the more.

"The Sparesons were all but wiped out at Gatekeeper rock. Those who survived were injured. They're no threat to you."

"Yet you survived, and young Bones. I'm of a mind to thinking there are more."

Charlie looked at Camilla as he considered his answer. She was no longer cursing him, but the look in her eyes was just as cruel; a look of disgust. "They could be anywhere," he said; his voice no longer strong and staunch, but faltering, like a reprimanded child.

"As I see it, I have barely enough men to be running errands. If I loose any more my friend who waits so anxiously for news of my well-being might not get his message." Elmshall revelled in his cruelty, struggling not to grin from the power he wielded over Charlie.

Charlie looked away. It was a conversation he wanted over. He began to walk back to the rock he had sat beneath earlier in the night, not for the shelter, as the rain had all but stopped, but because there he was unlikely to be bothered by anybody else, and he couldn't see the women.

He walked deliberately past the fire, but avoided eye contact with the women. He stooped down as he passed and picked up a piece of charred wood, without slowing his pace, such was his hurry to be out of sight.

For just a few seconds, it appeared to the men that the show was over. Those of a mind to sleeping began to crawl back under their blankets and the most vile of the Frenchmen, returned to the fireside, to goad the women.

"What the bloody hell was that?" Elmshall yelled. Hurrying to more open ground for a view of the sea, suspecting cannon fire.

"It's the town, Sir. At the harbour," the French lookout called from his post, on the track.

"Captain," Elmshall bellowed. "Your dead man has just blown the revenue." He was rattled. Angry. Hissing as he spoke. "Prepare to move at dawn," he bellowed. "And signal the Thorn."

"Then we both need to pray," Charlie said glumly, stopping in his paces, at the edge of the camp.

"No, Captain, we don't. In the morning we will be boarding the Thorn for a destination you don't need to know... You Captain, will be going out to find your little friend and you will kill him. That is all that will keep your family alive, now."

Charlie looked back at him with contempt. "By morning, he will be here." He spoke loudly; his words designed to spook the Frenchmen, whom he considered to be cowards.

"I'd wager you fought well in that village, Captain. Hoping to do enough to make me magically disappear." Elmshall spoke to him with a level of contempt and hatred that Charlie hadn't seen in him before. "That's what you do, isn't it; soldiers like you, that's what you're told. Stand and fight well and it'll all be alright. Except it probably won't be... Is that what you told the Sparesons when you led them to their death, in Spain?"

Charlie considered his reply. The heavy loses taken by the Sparesons at the Gatekeeper rock were an open wound that kept him awake at night and Elmshall instinctively knew it. "You asked me earlier, what became of the surviving Sparesons. Well they're out there; three of them, and don't expect this bunch of scurvy ridden blaggards to keep them from you. Not now." He pointed again at Camilla, to make his point.

"Major, Sir," one of the only remaining Welshmen amongst them gasped, having ran back from the town. "It was the Thorn, Sir. The Thorn robbed the revenue and blew up the stores."

Charlie smirked. "You're rats in a barrel," he said, continuing towards his rock, no longer caring what Elmshall said. "Sleep well, Major."

"Damn it man, are you sure?" Elmshall bellowed.

"Sure as I'm standing here, Sir... Begging your pardon, Sir, but the crew were getting restless, about the passengers, Sir." The Welshman gestured sheepishly towards the Frenchmen.

"Captain Magnusson wouldn't allow such a thing, restless or not."

"I doubt the Captain had a choice in the matter, Sir... She's changed her flag, Sir."

"What to, man?"

"A a different one, Sir," he stammered. "A a drunken man's banner, Sir. Not something Captain Magnusson would allow."

"Nobody sleeps." Elmshall boomed. "I want a line of defence a hundred yards forwards of here... I'll see any man flogged who lets a single soul through it."

Chapter 22

It had been the hardest thing, to wait for dawn, but Jack knew there was nothing he could do in the darkness. He knew Elmshall would be expecting him. That was the whole point of abducting the women in the first place; to force a mistake.

The night had barely given way to the dullness of the autumn dawn, when Jack made his move. It was the only course of action that he could envisage gaining any sort of victory, though there was so many things that could go wrong.

"Elmshall," he called, standing to the side of the track, behind a sturdy tree trunk, to avoid a lucky musket shot. "Major Elmshall." There was no immediate reply. He heard movements amongst the rocks and bushes, ahead. "Elmshall," he called again. "You can wait it out if you'd rather. It's quite a fortress you have here, but just remember, all the time you are waiting, the riders we have sent, will be getting closer to the border garrison. They're not many, but they're enough." Still only silence came from the camp. "You Frenchmen. Do you ever wonder what the worth is, of this Englishman that leads you to your death, from the rear... Us common men, we have a name for that kind of officer. Men that will send their men to their deaths and hide behind their corpses. They're bloody cowards... That is what you are, isn't it, Major; a coward."

Jack listened to every movement. Rustling leaves, a breaking twig. Every sound gave away the location of one of Elmshall's men amongst the heavy cover, in front of him.

"There's three of you. You're not going to hold us for long," Elmshall eventually called back, his voice clearly a considerable way behind the forward defences.

"You've nowhere to go, not now. We can hold you long enough." Jack called back, whilst beckoning for Cravith to move forwards and join him.

"You're missing the point, young Bones. I know you are three because your Captain told me you are."

Jack didn't reply at first. He looked back at Cravith. The exchange of glances spoke so many words. Just as he was beginning to doubt them, Jack's suspicions had been confirmed.

"He knows nothing of us... We've known for a while, not to trust him. He's a Lahand for pity's sake, why would we trust him." It was the best bluff jack could come back with, off the cuff, and it was largely true, but he felt a mistake had been made; the information Charlie had given Elmshall was accurate. "Your situation hasn't changed. You're boxed in with nowhere to go and your men are going to pay the price."

"The first to die will be the women. One of them is yours, Captain Halfbasket tells me. So, what are we to do?"

"You could wait it out. You never know, your men might not all be hung as spies, but we both know your fate, or of course we could take a less bloody course of action."

"What have you in mind, boy?"

"A duel. Just you and me, on the track."

Elmshall laughed loudly. "Have you ever even fought a duel, boy?"

"No, and I know you have. The best in England, so they tell me." Jack spoke boldly, knowing Elmshall would be under pressure from his own men to accept. "If I win, your men get a head start; enough time to steal a boat and make a run for it, and the women are released."

"And when I win?" Elmshall said in a spirit of humour.

"Exactly the same!"

"I don't think so, boy. Duels are fought between gentlemen. Gutter rats just shoot there opponents in the back."

"And if my second were a gentleman; a lord, even?"

"I'll shoot him myself if he fires a moment too soon," Cravith called back.

"If you're so keen to die, we'd better get on with it," Elmshall boomed joyfully. "There is one amendment to your proposal... You die and the women come with us."

"I have no intention of dying," Jack replied, trying, but failing to hide the concern from his voice.

Lord Cravith joined a Frenchman on the track, to measure out the distance; both Jack and Elmshall keeping out of sight until the distance had been agreed.

The Frenchman was an upright and smartly dressed man, quite unlike the rest of Elmshall's people, though not in uniform he was every bit an officer. "Regardless of the outcome, are we agreed that the other shall be given quarter to retreat?" he asked Cravith in perfect English and only a slight accent.

"You'll be given time to withdraw, but I should warn you that once you're off this hillside, you are at the mercy of the British army," Cravith said as the two met half way along the short section of straight track. "The distance is shorter, due to a limited field of battle. Is this acceptable to you?"

"It is, and the requirement for only a single pistol? I understand your man carries two."

"Mr bones will surrender one of his pistols before proceedings," Cravith assured him, beckoning Jack to step onto the track. "May God be with the righteous."

"Quite so," the Frenchman said, nodding his head as a matter of respect, before signalling for Elmshall to take his place on the narrow, tree lined track.

"Gentlemen. Due to circumstances, some of the usual protocols have been impossible, but I'm sure gentlemanly conduct will be adhered to, regardless of developments." Cravith took control of the proceedings with mutual agreement, his title of Lord making him the highest ranking gentleman present. "Upon my command, you will cock your pistols and fire. No man, under pain of death, will leave the field of battle until honour has been satisfied. Do you both understand."

"I do," Jack replied, while Elmshall remained silent, simply Nodding in agreement with a gleeful smirk on his face, the battle already being won, in his mind. "I do have a question, before we begin, as we're not both leaving here... What was it all about? What did you hope to gain by bringing a fist full of Frogs onto British soil?"

Elmshall smiled. "We've already achieved it!.. Shall we proceed?"

"Achieved what?" Jack asked with frustration.

"Control!" he said with a broadening grin.

"Gentlemen. Fire when ready," Cravith ordered, stepping back from the line of fire.

Jack stood square on, steadily raising his pistol for a sure aim. It wasn't the way a duel was generally fought, providing a wide target for his opponent. Upon Cravith's order, Elmshall cocked his pistol and raised it to a firing position in remarkably quick time, firing before Jack's pistol was even half way up.

Elmshall grinned as Jack fell, looking back at the Frenchman to receive praise for the perfect heart shot, that he had delivered. "You have five minuted before we come for you."

"My man hasn't fired yet," Cravith said calmly as Jack began to move.

"What trickery is this?" Elmshall demanded, his face losing every bit of colour at the prospect of receiving fire. He looked back at the Frenchman, who stood staunchly behind him, but out of the line of fire.

"It's a matter of honour, Sir," The French officer insisted, suspecting he may withdraw.

Elmshall looked back. Jack was struggling to his feet; clearly injured, but just as clearly, able to shoot.

"Sir, I must insist," the officer said, drawing his pistol, but before he could even cock it, Elmshall had drawn his sword and swiped it across his stomach. The French officer dropped to his knees; immobilised by the wound.

As Elmshall ran into the thorn trees, Jack fired, but it was hurried, his aim clouded by disorientation and pain.

"Did I get him?" Jack spluttered as he gasped for breath and fell back onto the track.

"I Don't know," Cravith replied glumly, pulling open Jack's jacket and shirt, to remove the civil war breast plate, which had been punctured by the shot.

With the first shot, Charlie had moved from his rock, waiting anxiously in close proximity to the women. Neither he nor Elmshall's men had any view of the fight. The first any one of them was to know of it when someone emerged from the track.

He bobbed down by the smouldered embers of the fire, as if to warm his hands. Camilla looked at him with the same contempt, but instinct told her not to draw attention to his actions.

"They have my wife and daughter," he whispered, sliding her the letter he had received, with the lock of their hair still stuck to it. "Give it to Jack. He has no reason to trust me, but I trust him... The address, where they are being held is on the back."

She held her silence, discretely looking at the letter with the charcoal writing on the back. She slipped it under the folds of her dress and looked back at him, still considering whether to trust him. She looked at his face in more detail. He was a troubled man. His face was racked with worry and guilt, and his eyes were filled with tears.

He looked around the camp. Every man was waiting to see who emerged, every pair of eyes were looking away. He drew his sword and cut the rope. "Run, hide, do what you have to," he said, pushing his sword into the earth beside him. "Please ask Jack, if he can find it in his heart to remember me as a friend."

"I never doubted you, and Jack never wanted to," she said with tears in her eyes as she dragged Estelle to her feet.

As the women scrambled amongst the rocks, the men began to cheer to the sight of Elmshall appeared from the track, limping with a shot wound to the thigh, but otherwise uninjured.

Before Elmshall was even in the camp, one of the Frenchmen noticed the women missing and raised his musket, only to be shot by Charlie with a musket that had been left unattended.

Every man looked from the edge of the camp, there reactions slowed by their lack of understanding of what was happening. Their returning fire was delayed by there assumption that Charlie was on their side, allowing him a clear pistol shot at another of them, who promptly dropped face down in full view.

As the muskets were trained on him, Charlie drew his sword from the earth and charged forwards, at two men, who were standing together, making him a moving shot for all but them. For them he should have been an easy target, though a terrifying one.

Both men shot hurriedly, and both shots hit him, but from the pure fear it wasn't the clean kill it should so easily have been. Charlie carried on, driven by the adrenaline pumping though his veins and liberated by the knowledge that his course was set and survival was no longer a goal.

With two swipes of his sword, both men dropped to the floor, mortally wounded. So many shots had been fire. So many empty muskets. With the desire to finish the job, six men ran forwards with swords and cutlasses, not taking the time to reload. Charlie thrashed at the wall of Frenchmen, who were scrambling to deliver the fatal blow, upon the enemy who had walked amongst them. With every swing of his sword, he struck flesh, and in turn a sword would stab or cut him.

The six had dwindled down to three injured men, before those who had taken the time to reload their muskets, ran in behind them, firing three shots into Charlie's already hopelessly wounded body, killing him on the spot.

"Fetch the women," Elmshall bellowed as he hobbled into the camp to see them gone. "Damn your eyes, them whores are our way out of here." He pranced forwards, scanning the rocky cliff-face for signs of them. "You three. Finish off the Bones boy and the Welsh Lord," he instructed the men, who had just shot Charlie.

The three stood and looked around them. They didn't immediately react to his order. "We are few now, Sir," one of them said in his poor English.

Elmshall was too concerned for the whereabouts of the women to notice their insubordination. "After them, I say," he shouted frantically as he began to climb the rocks, towards the seaward side.

"It's over, Major," came the voice of Bart Baker from the rocks ahead. Elmshall stood, exposed on the jagged rocks, and unable to move quickly, due to his poor footing.

"Are you the priest or the drunk?.. The late Captain told me all about you, you see."

"I was a priest!" Bart replied with Jack's rifle trained on Elmshall's chest.

Elmshall smiled. "Then surely you understand that it is only for God to take a life." As his words left his mouth, a shot rang out; not the loud bang of a musket, but the more subdued pop of a pistol.

Elmshall feel over sideways; a look of surprise and terror on his face as he stumbled off from the rocks, down the steep rocky hillside, before his lifeless body became wedged in the rocks, below.

Bart eventually refocused his attention on the camp, where the French officer stood with his discharged pistol, still pointing in the Bart's general direction, while every other man there, stood still, pointing their weapons to the ground, in a gesture of truce.

The officer stood doubled over with his arm across his bloodstained stomach. He shouted out an order in French, to which each of his men laid their weapons down. He placed his pistol in the dirt, in front of him and looked straight at Bart in an unspoken offer of surrender.

The sight he was seeing mesmerised Bart for a moment. He didn't immediately take his aim off of the officer, not because he had any other plans, but because he was utterly overwhelmed. Once more, he had found himself amongst the killing. Surrounded by death and clutching a rifle.

His failure to stand down quickly, caused a moment's tension amongst the Frenchmen, who stood with their gaze fixed, not just on Bart, but the entire hillside, expecting, as the seconds passed, that they would be shot on the spot from any direction.

"Mr Baker," Cravith called, appearing from the thorn trees, behind the officer. "Jack's been shot." Only then did Camilla appear from the rocks behind Bart, followed by Estelle.

By the time the three had scrambled through the rocks to the camp, the officer was stretched out on the floor, being tended to by his men. Bart gave him a long look as he carried on past, where as both Estelle and Camilla looked straight ahead, mercilessly denying his existence.

"You bloody mad fool," Bart said angrily, to the sight of Jack sprawled out on the track. "You're not going to keep getting away this sort of stupidity, you do know that, don't you?"

"Could have done with a bit more distance. Must make a note for next time," Jack gasped through the pain as Bart began to prod the wound.

"This is going to hurt, but I'm bloody sure you enjoy that." Bart produced from his pocket a pair of pincers and a round ended knife. "It's sitting on a rib... Ladies, one on each arm and a hand on his forehead."

First, with the knife, he attempted to loosen the shot, causing Jack excruciating pain and causing him to jump and fight as his body reacted in a series of involuntary motions.

"Jack, you must stay still," Camilla whispered, stroking his head.

"You must, or I'll stab you through the heart, myself," Bart said with conviction. "I'm going to give it a tug," he muttered as he pushed the pincers into shot hole, causing every muscle in Jack's body to tense. Estelle pushed a stick across Jack's mouth, for him to bite on, just as the pain began to intensify. "All your strength, ladies," he instructed, before pulling upwards, downwards, then straight out, all in the space of three seconds.

Chapter 23

"The Lady Gull is in harbour at the moment. Captain and crew will be in the alehouse by noon," Cravith explained to the French officer, who laid outstretched on a makeshift stretcher. His chanced of ever seeing France again were slim, and both men knew it. They also knew that he was the only leadership the remaining Frenchmen had, and without his command, they would surely never leave British soil.

"What about me? I can't go to France," a Welsh voice spoke from beside the officer.

Cravith's face instantly filled with anger at the realisation that one of the survivors was Welsh. "No you can't," he said, punching the man full on the jaw. "You'll hang, either as a traitor or a smuggler, that is the only choice left open for you."

The French officer nodded solemnly, in acceptance of the fact that the man was worse than himself; not a spy, but a traitor to his country.

Cravith shook the officer's hand as a fellow gentlemen and leader of men. Jack had explained to Cravith that it was better for the country, if those men were never caught. The notion of them being a few foreign smugglers, washed up on a remote shore, would allow the people to go about their business, without the panic and unrest that a French military incursion would undoubtedly have caused.

Jack had promptly disobeyed Bart's instruction, to remain still. He didn't feel he could. Clutching his chest and the thick wad of cloth he had as a bandage, he made his way to Charlie's body. "Help me with him, will you," he called to Cravith, as the Frenchmen began to leave the camp. "He shouldn't have to lay with them." Jack was struggling to pull Charlie's body from amongst the men he had killed, while Camilla struggled, quite ineffectively to help, gagging at the sight of some of the sword wounds and most specifically the shot wound which had take the back off of Charlie's head.

Before Cravith even got to him, Jack sat down on a log; exhausted, not by his efforts, but by his loss of blood.

"Rest, man, or you'll be joining him," Cravith said, distracted by Bart, who was making his way towards the sea, past the jagged rocks where Elmshall's body had become wedged.

"As a Lord of this land, I believe you would be able to file a military report for the action, here, today?"

"I can. Of course," Cravith replied, his focus still on Bart's progression along the cliffs.

"Let it be recorded that Captain Charles Halfbasket died with honour and courage, in service of his King and his Country." Camilla sat beside him, wrapping her arms around his waist, both as a matter of affection and to dissuade him from attempting to move any further.

"For whatever reason, he may have lost his way, but he was shown the light, at the end," Cravith said, as he pulled Charlie's gruesomely battered body away from the other corpses.

"Lord Cravith, Sir," Estelle called ahead, as she led six armed men from the town, into the camp. "These men heard shooting, Sir. They've come to help," She explained.

"Very much appreciated, gentlemen, but I'm rather afraid you've missed all the fun," Cravith said, glancing back instinctively, to see the Frenchmen had all left the camp.

"I'm sure there's more of us on the way, Sir, but with the revenue having been blown up, nobody knows what to do," the tubby, well dressed man, explained. He kicked the foot of one of the Frenchmen. "At least you gentlemen managed to corner a few of em. We didn't see hide nor hair."

"A banker, is it?" Jack asked, looking up from his log, at the self important little man.

"Yes, Sir, I am of that profession."

"Thought so. It must be the smell of other people's money that gives it away, every time."

The man huffed, while the five men behind him sniggered or smirked, irritating him further.

"Thing is, I heard a different story, but we mustn't listen to stories must we," Jack said cheerfully.

"Oh, I think stories are very important. Gets us through the grim winter's evenings," Cravith said with a smile, following Jack's lead.

"Well, a labourer friend of mine, claims you and your brave bunch of volunteers were gathered on a back street, the whole time, while the revenue stores were being emptied... But then he was just a labourer. What would he know?"

"I can assure you," the tubby man began, before Jack interrupted.

"Relax. Nobody is going to listen to a humble labourer, no more than they are going to listen, when he suggests that the whole crooked crowd of you waited in that back street, because you assumed it was another one of Mr Winter's cargo's arriving," Jack's voice gradually changed, giving way to his anger for Charlie's death.

"My Lord, I must object," the tubby man protested, while the other five men seemed to shrink, stepping back or looking around the camp.

"I think today might be best served cleaning house, Sir. A lot of filth been blowing about in last night's storm," Cravith said, cryptically. "I think you'll find his majesty will be sending South Wales a new broom!"

The tubby man went instantly pale, looking back at the men behind him. "Sir," he muttered, no longer feeling able to look either Jack nor Cravith in the eye.

"Sirs. What is that man doing?" one of the other men asked, watching Bart, who had made his way as far around the rock-face as he could. He stood on the edge, looking down at the sea below, as it lashed the jagged rocks.

"Mr Baker," Cravith shouted desperately, while Estelle seemed to freeze.

Bart looked back at them in an almost unworldly manner. It was a picture that had the potential to stay with each of them forever, as he slowly waved and stepped forwards, calmly plummeting from sight.

The six townsmen rushed forwards, beginning the slow climb through the rocks, to reach the point he had jumped from. As Cravith tried to join them, Jack grabbed his hand. "I think your villages have just gained their doctor," he whispered, smiling briefly, just to let Cravith know all was not as it seemed.

Cravith looked across at Estelle, who looked no more than mildly concerned. She looked around at him and bowed her head slightly, as if to assure him.

"Careful, gentlemen. Those rocks are deadly," Cravith called, attempting to buy Bart a few extra seconds, to get out of sight. "If he went in there, he's a dead man."

"Why would he?" one of the townsmen asked, genuinely troubled by what he had witnessed.

"Father Baker was a troubled man," Jack said sombrely. "He had witnessed some ungodly things."

"He was a Priest?" the man said in astonishment. "Isn't that damnation?"

"That Priest was damned, anyway," Cravith added, gesturing towards Estelle.

"Tenby has seen some peculiar sorts of late, Sir," the man said, shaking his head as he made his way back from the rocks, having lost all interest in Bart's fate.

Cravith found an old sack, left behind by Elmshall's men. He draped it over Charlie's mutilated body. "You can leave the others for the crows for all me, but this man needs to be returned to England," he instructed the tubby man, who nodded sheepishly, his thoughts engulfed by the investigation that would surely follow the events, there and in the town.

Jack was clutching the letter Charlie had left, apparently reading it again and again. "What are you going to do about that?" Cravith asked as he sat down beside Jack and Camilla.

Jack looked at Camilla. For once in his life, he didn't want to venture or travel, he only wanted to be by her side, to protect her. "It could all be a rotten trick. She was a traitor, you know."

"Charlie was believing it," Camilla said, her English muddling as happened when she was upset. "He gave life up, for us, and for them," she said as tears began to run down her face. "We must go. Me and you."

"No," Jack said firmly. "You have seen too much of all this." He took from his neck the whale bone lighthouse pendant and handed her it. "Take this to the Bone house and they will look after you; forever, if that's how long it takes."

She pushed it away. "That's your luck, Jack. You always said it."

"If it keeps you safe, that's all the luck I need."

She kissed him full on the lips; her tears soaking his face. As Jack reached around her waist and began to lower his hand, Cravith stood up and deliberately coughed, falsely, causing Jack to stop abruptly.

"We will of course see Mr Dewson back to health... He was awake and talking, when I left... With Meryl!"

"He's a good man, Sir. You couldn't want for better."

"This land has lost a lot of good men, to King George's warring. Our women have, too."

"Maybe you can show him a new fight," Camilla interrupted, her face full of hope that something other than death, might come out it all.

"By God's will. I won't stand in their way," Cravith agreed.

Chapter 24

As Jack rode, in search of a ship for America, two riders were entering London. They rode the streets boldly and purposefully, considering their cargo to be of the uttermost importance.

As they approached the palace grounds, and specifically the cottage of Thomas Verance, one man stopped and dismounted. As his companion continued to ride, he stood, boldly watching the guard, on the gate.

"Important dispatch for Mr Thomas Verance," the rider declared to the guard, before handing an unimpressive twice folded letter, wax sealed with Verance's own personal seal, used only by the Verance family, back in Norfolk.

The guard immediately suspected something unusual. The two men seemed to be on edge, looking to each other intermittently, as if something hugely significant was about to happen.

"Lincoln," the guard called to a second man, a few yards inside the gate. He brought his musket to the most ready position he could, without actually pointing it at the man.

"I'm sure you'll find everything in order... I'm to await a response."

The guard handed the letter over his shoulder, to Lincoln, without breaking eye contact. "For Mr Verance."

He looked down the street to see that the second man was back on his horse, trotting away. "You may be waiting a while. A very busy man, is Mr Verance."

"I don't think I'll have long to wait," the man replied, looking down at his feet, as if to ovoid giving anything away in his facial expression.

Lincoln hurried to the cottage door and surrendered his musket to the two guards. This was a new protocol, brought about in the light of a series of recent events, surrounding men of power and influence.

He knocked on the internal door, to the room, which Verance had seldom left, in recent days.

"Come in," Verance replied, upturning a document on his desk as a matter of routine.

"Hand delivered, to the gate, Sir," Lincoln said, placing the letter in his hand. "By an unknown hand, Sir."

"My wife's seal," Verance said with an air of concern. "That will be all."

"Sir. The rider awaits a reply."

Verance, at first ignored him as he broke the seal. Without reading a word, the two locks of hair, waxed to the letter, told him all he needed to know. He looked up at Lincoln; not as a passing glance, but as a fixed stare, absorbing all of his concentration.

"You will have your response, Mr Lincoln. Now kindly wait outside. I'm not to be disturbed."

He looked at the letter; still not reading the words. He already knew what was required of him. He touched the hair with his index finger, knowing that was as near to his wife and daughter as he would ever get.

Eventually he read the words, just to confirm, beyond all doubt, its requirements.

He placed the letter on the desk and looked up at the painting of the harbour, which had represented the best of his life. For a moment, in his mind, he could imagine himself back there; standing, watching his ship come in, with his wife and daughter by his side.

He tried to fix that image in his head as he opened his desk draw. He imagined the sound of gulls squabbling over the fishtails, on the quayside and dockers banter, as his cargo was brought to shore.

Still with his eyes fixed on the painting, he cocked his pistol. It was as if he was with them. He couldn't see the pistol, he made sure it was out of his view. Only as the barrel touched the side of his head, did he allow himself to accept it was there.

As he closed his eyes, he squeezed the trigger, ending the life of one of the country's most influential and powerful men.

Thank you for taking an interest in the Rib Bone Jack series and I hope you will continue to follow Jack's adventures. If you enjoyed the books, could I ask that you take a moment to leave a short review. By doing this, readers can truly take control of what is written in the future and encourage the popularity of their favourite works, taking that power from the hands of the all-powerful publishing companies, who have ruled literature for so long.

If you liked this, why not have a look at my new series, Legacy of the Rhino. The first two books are available now.
https://www.amazon.com/dp/B07MC55PNV